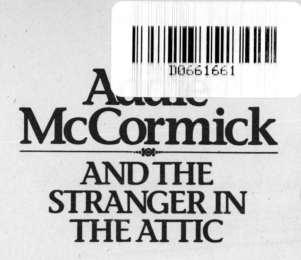

Addie McCormick

AND THE STRANGER IN THE ATTIC

Leanne Lucas

HARVEST HOUSE PUBLISHERS
Eugene, Oregon 97402

Addie McCormick and the Stranger in the Attic

Copyright © 1992 by Leanne Lucas
Published by Harvest House Publishers
Eugene, Oregon 97402

Library of Congress Cataloging-in-Publication Data

Lucas, Leanne, 1955-
    Addie McCormick and the stranger in the attic   /
Leanne Lucas.
        p. cm. — (Addie adventure series ; bk. 1)
        Summary: Addie learns new lessons about Christian
    life when she and Nick try to help an elderly neighbor
    and uncover a mystery surrounding a strange visitor, a
    hidden room, and a secret past.
        ISBN 1-56507-052-6
        [1. Mystery and detective stories. 2. Old age—
    Fiction.
    3. Christian life—Fiction.]   I. Title.   II. Series:
    Lucas, Leanne.   1955-   Addie adventure series ; bk. 1
    PZ7.L96963Ae   1992
    [Fic]—dc20   92-2234
                                                         CIP
                                                         AC

Printed in the United States of America.

CHAPTER 1

The Stranger

The light of the television glowed softly in the dimly lit room. Addie sat and watched as Monica lay limply in Gerald's arms. The woman's voice grew weaker with every breath. Tears streamed down Gerald's face, and Addie reached for another tissue.

"Oh, Gerald, I've loved you so much," Monica moaned.

"And I, you, darling," Gerald choked out.

"Never forget the wonderful life we've shared," Monica said, her eyes fluttering shut. "Promise me."

"Never," Gerald whispered. "I'll love you forever."

An angelic smile crossed Monica's face and her eyes closed one last time. She gave a delicate little shudder and then lay still.

Gerald and Addie both sobbed as a gentle, shimmering light illuminated Monica's face. The picture faded and Addie flopped back on the sofa, exhausted. She reached for the last tissue and blew her nose hard. Mrs. McCormick stood in the door of the living room, shaking her head and smiling at her sentimental, eleven-year-old daughter.

"No one will ever love me like that," Addie sighed.

"I hope not!" her mother exclaimed with a laugh. "Real life is much better than the movies. And that one must be at least 40 years old."

"Yeah," Addie said. "They sure don't make 'em like they used to, do they?"

"Really, Addie, you've been watching too much television." Mrs. McCormick frowned. Addie knew what was coming next.

"Why don't you turn it off and go outside and get some exercise?"

Addie heaved herself off the couch and picked up the empty tissue box. "It's kind of gloomy out. Can't I just go upstairs and finish my book?" If anything appealed to Mrs. McCormick more than exercise, it was reading. She thought every child should be made to read at least one hour a day, summer vacation or not. But this time exercise won out.

"Later," she said. "Now you need to get out. It's not gloomy. It's perfectly beautiful. Nice and cool. Go on, now." She gave Addie a motherly push toward the door.

"I know what I can do," Addie said. "I'll take my bike and ride the four-mile square. Maybe I can stop and meet the old lady who lives close to the main road." She paused. "Everybody at church says she's a strange old bird."

"Addie!" her mother exclaimed. "I don't want you calling anyone a 'strange old bird.' That's rude. She's probably a very nice woman."

"Well, there's something different about her. The kids say she won't let anyone in her house. When she sees people coming, if she's in the yard she runs back in the house and won't talk to them."

"Then how do you plan to meet her?" her mother asked.

"Oh, I'll just sneak up on her," Addie answered as she ducked into the kitchen. She threw the tissue box in the trash and ran out the back door before her mother could stop her. Grabbing her bike from against the garage wall, she mounted it and pedaled through the grass into the driveway. The screen door opened and Mrs. McCormick called,

"Addie, be polite!"

"I *will* , Mother," Addie yelled over her shoulder.

Addie was always polite. Well, almost always. At least, she tried to be. Sometimes things just popped out of her mouth before she knew it and people thought she was trying to be smart. She wasn't, though; she just hadn't learned to think before she spoke. Her father always quoted Proverbs 21:23 at those times. "He who guards his mouth and his tongue keeps himself from calamity." He even made Addie memorize it, with the hope that when she started to say something she shouldn't, she would think of that verse first. Sometimes it worked. Then again, sometimes it didn't. That's when she got in trouble.

Well, today would be different. If she got the chance to talk to Miss Tisdale (the old lady), her mouth would drip honey. If there was a mystery she was hiding, Addie wanted to be the one to discover it. All the kids at church thought there was something strange going on in that house. If Addie could find out what it was, the summer wouldn't be a complete bust.

As it was, the summer had been pretty boring so far. The McCormicks had moved from Wisconsin to Illinois at the beginning of June. Their large old farmhouse sat surrounded by corn and bean fields. It was a nice home and the land was pretty (if you liked corn and beans), but the nearest house was over a mile away and vacant. Addie had learned at church a new family was moving in this week. Maybe they'd have a girl her age. Then again, maybe they'd have a boy and he'd be a creep. Why was it all the boys her age were usually creeps? It was only in the movies that you'd find one interesting and fun to be with. They just didn't come that way in real life.

Addie came up on the vacant house, and sure enough, there was a moving van sitting in the driveway. Several people were milling in and out, carrying large boxes and crates. Addie strained to see some sign of a girl. There were two large men— the movers, probably—a woman with a baby, and a man. Then two skinny legs swung down from the back of the van and Addie held her breath.

A boy. He watched Addie approach the house, so she stood up and pedaled faster, zipping by without looking at him. Then she couldn't help but glance back. He was still watching, so she turned around and pedaled furiously. Her long black hair streamed out behind her. She didn't slow down until she reached the corner.

A boy. Well, at least it was another kid. He looked okay, but then you could never tell just by looks. He might be one of those boys that liked to punch girls on the arm every chance he got and show off a lot. If he was, there was no way Addie was going to be friends with him. Her mother thought it was important to be friends with your neighbors. Since this was the closest house within a mile, that probably qualified the people moving into it as neighbors. Still, Addie wasn't going to be friends with that boy unless she wanted to.

She rode slowly, thinking of all the things she wanted to do and couldn't. She couldn't see the kids from her church because they lived in town and Addie didn't. She couldn't belong to the youth group because her family only had one car and her father needed it. He was the manager of a Christian radio station 30 miles in the opposite direction of town and the church. And she couldn't even complain about all the things she couldn't do. Her father said God provided everything she needed and she had to be thankful. She *was* thankful, but she just wished God would provide what she *wanted* sometimes, not just what she *needed*.

Like right now. What she wanted was to meet Miss Tisdale and find out she had a deep dark secret no one else knew about. It would add some mystery to the summer, and probably make all the other kids jealous. The idea of being the envy of all her new friends made her pedal faster.

In a few minutes Miss Tisdale's big, three-story house loomed ahead. Addie's heart began to pound. She wasn't scared, but she began to wish she had a friend with her. Even that new kid would be a help. Her friends had told her so many weird things about Miss Tisdale, she began to believe them as she got nearer to "the mansion."

It was called the mansion because it must have been a beautiful house when it was first built at the turn of the century. There were a half-dozen large pillars that lined the veranda on the first floor. The second floor windows went from the floor to the ceiling and opened out into individual patios. The third floor windows were small and very dark. Some of the panes were cracked or broken, and not all of them had curtains. The whole house needed a paint job. It was obvious it no longer got the attention it needed to be a real mansion.

Addie was tempted to ride by the way she had every other time this summer, but something made her put on the brakes. She stopped at the end of the graveled drive that wound past the mansion to the empty greenhouse at the back of the yard.

A slight breeze tickled the back of Addie's neck and she shivered. Although it was the middle of July, it was cool. The sun was hidden in a cloud-filled sky that made a gloomy backdrop for the old grey house. There was no sign of life. Addie's courage began to ebb. "Sneaking up" on Miss Tisdale

was a more serious task than it h
safety of her own living room.

Suddenly something moved in
floor windows. Addie pedaled past the di...
stopped behind the hedge row that lined the front
yard. She dropped her bike and it clattered to the
ground. Ducking behind the hedge, she waited a
few moments, then peered cautiously over the top
of the bushes.

The third-floor window was empty, but the curtain fluttered as if it had just been disturbed. Addie remained motionless, waiting for some sign of the old woman. An eternity passed and nothing happened. Just as she began to relax, her glance strayed to the other end of the house and her heart jammed into her throat. There, in the last window, a man in a grey raincoat stood staring straight at her!

Addie dropped to her knees behind the hedge, scrunched as close to the ground as her long legs would let her and squeezed her eyes shut. *Maybe he didn't see me. Maybe he didn't know I was watching him. Maybe   maybe frogs will fly tomorrow!*

A man in Miss Tisdale's attic? Everyone knew she lived alone in the mansion. Addie's friends had mentioned a niece that came to visit once in a while, but never a nephew or even a male friend. And why was he there? Surely Miss Tisdale didn't take visitors up to a third-floor attic that had broken windows and—

"What do you think you're doing?" a rough voice growled. Addie whipped around, burning her knees on the grass, expecting the worst.

CHAPTER 2

A New Neighbor

"I said, what do you think you're doing?" The new boy stood behind her, feet apart, arms folded across his chest. He had blond hair that curled damply on his forehead in the humid weather, and his eyes were brown. He was scowling as if he'd just seen a crime committed.

"What business is it of yours?" Addie snapped. She stood up and rubbed her knees to take away some of the sting. She glanced back at the house. The window was empty. "I don't have to explain anything to you. Who are you, anyway?"

"Nicholas Brady," he answered and the scowl turned to a smile. "Yeah, you're right. You don't have to explain anything to me. But when you whizzed past on your bike, I could tell you were up to something. Since I was getting bored with moving boxes, I thought I'd follow you and see why you were in such a hurry."

"So why'd you yell at me just now?" Addie's deep blue eyes narrowed. She was still wary of Nicholas Brady.

11

"Oh, that," he answered. "I talk like that to everyone I meet for the first time. I figure anyone I can bully isn't worth my trouble." He grinned again. "But you seem like you can hold your own. What's your name?"

"Addie."

"Addie what?"

"Addie McCormick."

"So, what's going on?"

"Well..." Addie hesitated, reluctant to share a "mystery" that might not seem so mysterious to this brash new kid.

"Come on," he prodded. "I know there's something strange going on. You dropped to the ground like you'd seen a ghost."

Addie nodded. "Someone was standing in that window," she pointed to the third floor, "watching me."

"Why shouldn't they watch you?" he hooted. "You're spying on them, aren't you?"

"No!" she protested. "I came to meet old Miss Tisdale. There was a man in the window."

"Well, does she have a husband?"

Addie shook her head and spoke slowly. "That's why they call her *Miss* Tisdale."

Nicholas ignored the sarcasm. "Any friends, nephews...?"

"Not that I know of."

"If you're just coming to meet her, how do you know there aren't any men in her family?"

"The kids at church told me. Everybody knows all about her, but no one's ever been able to meet her. She's a strange old bird," Addie said.

Nicholas frowned. "That's rude. You shouldn't call people names if you don't know what they're like."

"And then it's okay, I suppose?" Addie retorted.

"That's not what I meant!"

"You're certainly inconsistent," Addie sniffed. "You get offended when I call someone a name, but you give everyone you meet a 'bully' test to see if they're worth your time."

"You passed it, didn't you?" he shot back.

"I—I—" Addie sputtered a few syllables and clamped her mouth shut. They glared at one another for several seconds. Addie picked up her bike and began marching down the long drive. The gravel crunched behind her and Nicholas appeared on her left. She stared straight ahead, ignoring him.

"You're not going up there alone," he said.

"She's just an old lady," Addie scoffed.

"An old lady with somebody sneaking around her house," he reminded her. Addie slowed down just a little.

"Truce?" Nicholas stopped and stuck out his hand. Addie shook it.

"Truce," she said. There was an awkward silence as they started back up the drive. They walked up the steps to the front door. Nicholas spoke first.

"Who's going to do the talking?"

"Let—" *Let me*, she started to say, then thought better of it. "Let's just see how it goes," she said.

"Okay." He rapped sharply on the door and they waited. Several seconds passed. He knocked again, louder this time, and still no one answered.

"You don't suppose whoever I saw upstairs has hurt Miss Tisdale, do you?" Addie's voice cracked halfway through the sentence and dropped to a whisper. "What should we do?"

"I don't know," Nicholas whispered back. "Let's go around the side of the house and see if we can get in a window."

"That's trespassing," Addie protested.

"Not if she's hurt," he said. "Then we can call it 'coming to the aid of the elderly' or something like that."

Addie's expression mirrored her disapproval, but she followed him around the corner of the house and down the side yard to the back. Nicholas peered around the corner, and Addie poked her head over his shoulder. There was no one there, so they scurried up the steps to the back door. Nicholas peered cautiously through the screen and jumped back so fast he threw Addie against the side of the house and she hit her head.

They plastered themselves to the siding and waited in silence, breathing hard.

"Is she in there?" Addie mouthed.

Nicholas nodded. "She must be deaf as a post if she didn't hear you hit your head just then," he whispered back.

"It wasn't my fault," Addie began to argue, but Nicholas shook his head and clamped his hand over her mouth.

She opened it to bite him and he dropped his hand quickly. "Just be quiet, will you?" he hissed.

"Why?" Addie straightened up. "We haven't done anything wrong. We came here to meet her. So let's meet her."

She pushed past him and stepped in front of the screen door. In the middle of the kitchen a tall, thin woman stood with her back to them. Her thick grey hair was pulled into a bun. She wore an oversized apron draped over a purple-flowered dress. Several cardboard boxes sat on the table in front of her. She mumbled softly to herself as she stuffed crumpled newspaper into the only box still open. The screen door bounced under Addie's sharp tap.

Miss Tisdale spun around and picked up the glasses that hung on a chain around her neck. She walked briskly to the door and peered out through wire-rim bifocals.

"Yes?" Her thin, sharp voice crackled and Addie lost her nerve.

"Are . . . are you Miss Tisdale?"

"What?" She put her hand behind her ear and Addie repeated the question.

"Are you Miss Tisdale?"

"Yes, of course I am. Who else would I be?"

Nicholas nudged Addie to one side and smiled broadly. "Hi, Miss Tisdale. My name's Nicholas Brady and this is Addie McCormick. We're your neighbors."

Miss Tisdale looked the two children up and down, then fixed her stare on Nicholas' smiling face.

"I don't have any neighbors."

His smile faded. "Well, I don't mean right-next-door neighbors," he stammered. "But we're as close as you've got."

"Humpf," she said. "Where do you live?"

"We're just moving into the Lindseys' old place," he said, "and Addie . . . Addie . . ." he faltered and Addie spoke up.

"I live in the green, two-story house on route 49."

"Oh. The minister's family." She said minister like it was a bad word, and Nicholas looked at Addie in surprise. Addie just shrugged and stood up straighter. She was proud of being a preacher's kid and she wasn't going to let some old lady make her feel any different.

"Well. What do you want?" Miss Tisdale asked.

"We just thought we'd . . . we want to . . . I guess . . ." Now Nicholas was at a loss for words.

"We were just trying to be neighborly," Addie said shortly. "Sorry we bothered you. Come on, Nicholas."

Addie turned to leave, but Miss Tisdale opened the back door and motioned them in. "Did I say you were bothering me?" she asked. Addie shrugged again and Miss Tisdale put her hand on the young girl's shoulder and patted it roughly. "Come in, come in." The children stepped into the kitchen, sniffing at the rich smell of chocolate chip cookies that hung in the air.

"In my experience, neighborly usually means nosy," she went on, "but I haven't had company for quite a while. You might as well take a look around and satisfy your curiosity. That way maybe you won't 'bother' me anymore. Humph."

Nicholas and Addie exchanged a fearful glance. No company for quite a while? That meant the man upstairs was either family or . . . an uninvited guest.

Nicholas looked around nervously, noticing the boxes on the table. "What are you packing?" he asked. "Can we help? Are you mailing these somewhere? Is there someone here to pick them up? Is that why—?"

"It's none of your business what I'm packing," Miss Tisdale interrupted him, "and no, I don't need your help. No one is picking these up; they're going into the attic." She stuffed the remaining paper in the last box and closed it up quickly. She sat another box on top of it and carried them both to the stairwell on the far side of the kitchen. She continued stacking boxes as she talked.

"I suppose you're curious about my house. It seems every child in the county thinks there's some great mystery going on here. Just because a house is big and old doesn't mean there's anything mysterious about it. I've lived here for almost 45 years and every summer I get a new crop of nosy children trying to find their way inside. At least you had the decency to come to the door instead of trying to sneak in through some window."

Addie gave Nicholas an "I told you so" glance. "We'd never do that, Miss Tisdale," she said. "We just wanted to meet you. We thought you might appreciate the company. It must be lonely living here by yourself."

"Oh, I don't mind that a bit. I like my privacy. I have my niece and her family to visit me, although those visits aren't the most pleasant ones I've had lately." She shook her head as if she wanted to shake out bad memories. "Well, enough of that. I've got better things to think about."

"You live here by yourself, then?" Nicholas said and Miss Tisdale gave him a strange look.

"Yes, of course I do, child. Why do you ask?"

"You never have company?" he persisted.

"No, Mr. Brady, hardly ever!" she snapped.

"Then who—?"

"And," she interrupted again, "if you came snooping around here to see if those rumors about old Mr. Crenshaw and I are true, I'm afraid you're going to be disappointed. I'm too old to start going out with men again. There hasn't been a man courting me for years and there isn't about to be. You can tell that to your friends, and your enemies, and the whole county if you want to!"

She turned back to the table and picked up more boxes, stomping over to the stairwell and dropping them on the floor.

"What do we do now?" Addie mouthed to Nicholas. "We've got to ask her about—"

"What?" Miss Tisdale turned suddenly and fixed Addie with a stare. "What's the secret, miss?"

"I, well, I was just telling Nicholas I thought we ought to ask you if—" Addie swallowed hard and Miss Tisdale interrupted once more.

"Ask me if you can have one of those cookies, isn't that right? I thought I saw you eyeing them when you came in. Well, I guess I can spare one or two. I baked them just this morning. My niece and her boys are coming tomorrow and they enjoy my cookies. You probably will too. Humph."

Addie looked at Nick and shrugged helplessly. As Miss Tisdale reached for the cookie jar that sat on the counter behind her, there was a muffled thud from above the kitchen. Nicholas and Addie both jumped.

Miss Tisdale picked up the cookie jar as if she hadn't heard a thing.

"One each," she said.

CHAPTER 3

Lost in the Woods

A second, softer thud followed the first and the two children looked at Miss Tisdale expectantly.

"Well, do you want a cookie or not?" she snapped.

"Sure," Nicholas answered. He took the largest one he could see. Addie hesitated. How could Nicholas eat at a time like this? Then the aroma of chocolate drifted out of the jar and Addie reached in. Just one. After all, it was a sure bet Miss Tisdale wasn't going to make the offer a third time.

She was about to take a bite when a third thump made her freeze, mouth open, cookie in mid-air. Miss Tisdale continued to ignore the noise and sat the cookie jar back on the counter.

"What are we going to do?" Addie hissed softly.

Miss Tisdale turned around again and caught her in mid-whisper. "Why do you keep whispering behind my back?" She glared at Addie over her bifocals.

"We keep hearing noises upstairs, Miss Tisdale." Addie paused. "Can't you hear them?"

Miss Tisdale seemed to pale slightly, but her expression never changed. "Old houses make noises all the time, child. You should know that, you live in one. Of course I heard it, I—I just ignored it, that's all." She turned and picked up the last stack of boxes.

Addie glanced at Nick, but he was staring out the window. She followed his gaze and saw a tall figure dressed in a grey raincoat disappear into the woods that bordered the west side of the mansion.

"Well, we have to go now, Miss Tisdale," Nick said and stuffed the rest of his cookie in his mouth. He took Addie's arm and propelled her toward the door. "Thanks for the cookies."

"What's your hurry?" Miss Tisdale asked. Her back was to the window and she hadn't seen the man. "Do you always eat and run like this?"

"I promised my mom I wouldn't be gone long," Nicholas said. "Maybe we could stop by again tomorrow. Come *on* Addie," he said as he pushed her through the screen door.

Addie glared at him but allowed herself to be "helped" down the steps. "We'll come back soon, Miss Tisdale . . . that is, if you don't mind."

"I suppose I don't. It breaks the monotony of the day. Well, goodbye." She stepped back inside and the door banged shut.

Nicholas ran around the corner of the house and back toward the road.

"Where are you going now?" Addie called as she ran after him.

"After that man," Nick answered. He slowed to let Addie catch up and she grabbed his arm and pulled him to a stop.

"Nicolas, that's crazy. I think we should go back and tell Miss Tisdale that man was in her house. What if—?"

"Addie, she knew he was there! Didn't you see her face when you mentioned the noises? She just didn't want *us* to know she knew he was there."

"That doesn't make sense. And anyway, I don't agree with you. I think she was just embarrassed because she couldn't hear the noises and didn't want to admit it. Besides, if she knew he was there, why do we need to follow him? It's none of our business."

Nick shook his head. "Just because she knew he was there doesn't mean he was *supposed* to be there."

"And how do you know that?"

"If he was just paying a visit, why did he leave without saying goodbye? Why did he go through those woods? *Where's his car?*"

Addie didn't answer.

"Addie, something's going on and I want to find out what!"

The mystery Addie had longed for only an hour earlier was beginning to take shape, and it scared her. If Miss Tisdale was in danger, Addie wanted to help. But were they going to get involved in something they couldn't handle? Addie shivered.

"Come on," Nicholas urged. "We don't want Miss Tisdale to see us, so we'll pretend to leave, then sneak back around and into the woods."

Addie hesitated briefly, but finally followed him. After all, it *was* a mystery, wasn't it? How could she desert Nicholas now? If she did, it would be his ballgame all the way. She wasn't about to let him get all the credit for uncovering the secret of Miss Tisdale and her mysterious visitor.

They ran all the way around the house and into the back yard from the east side. Addie checked the window into the kitchen. Miss Tisdale was nowhere in sight, so they hurried into the woods. Nicholas began crashing through the underbrush.

"Nicholas," Addie called in a low voice. "At least use your head. If we're going to follow this guy, we had better do it the smart way."

Nicholas stopped and waited for Addie to catch up. "What do you mean? He's going to get away if we don't hurry."

He started off again, but Addie grabbed his arm. "If he hears us coming he's bound to hide. Or worse, he could turn on us and then who knows what he'd do? We have to be quiet. I think there's an easier way to get through these woods than tearing through the underbrush the way you were." Addie paused and looked around. "He went into the trees up there, didn't he?"

Nicholas nodded and the two began to pick their way through the woods carefully. "One of my friends told me there's a path through these trees that leads to the main road," Addie said. "He probably left his car on the road and walked through the woods. If we find that path, we might find him."

Nick nodded. "But I can't see anything—look! Over there!"

Addie strained to see what he was pointing at. There, laying on the ground, was a dark grey handkerchief. A few yards ahead was a well-worn path that meandered through the brush.

"Let's go!"

They began running through the woods, moving quickly now that they had found a clear path. Many minutes passed, and what began as an earnest race deteriorated into a half-hearted trot.

Nicholas finally stopped, holding his side. Addie stopped beside him and they both stood for a few seconds, gasping for breath.

"Are you sure this is the right path?" Nicholas asked.

"Of course I'm sure," she answered. "What else could it be?"

"Okay," he said. "But you better be right."

They started again, this time more slowly. They walked and walked . . . and walked. The path wasn't as clear as it had been at the start, and it seemed to wind around. Finally Nicholas stopped.

"Where are we?"

"We're on the path," Addie answered. "What's it look like?"

"It looks like we're going in circles and getting nowhere fast, that's what it looks like," he retorted.

"Then turn around and go back," she answered. "I'm going on. We've got to be getting close to the main road. I'm not giving up now."

Addie continued down the path and Nick followed. Underbrush and branches crowded them on both sides. Nicholas began to mumble and Addie said a silent prayer.

"Lord, get us out of this. I have no idea where we are, but you do. Do something, fast!" That sounded like a command, so she added a quick and fervent *"Please!"*

Just about that time, the path dwindled down to nothing and disappeared completely. Addie paused, looking into the tangled underbrush ahead. Nicholas stood beside her in the same pose she had seen when they first met—feet spread, arms folded across his chest.

"So now what do we do, Miss Detective?" he sneered.

Addie didn't answer. Nicholas started to rant and rave. "Boy, I don't believe this. How could you get us into this? 'Look for a path,' you said. 'Do it the smart way,' you said. Well, this is *real smart*. Now we're going to have to fight our way through that mess just to get back to the main road. Which way is it, anyway?"

Addie looked at him helplessly, and he finally caught on to what she had known for the last 10 minutes. They were lost.

His mouth dropped open and he stared at her bug-eyed. "Don't tell me—you mean you don't know—oh, brother!" He covered his face with his hands and sank to the ground. "I thought you knew what you were doing. How could you get us into this mess?"

"Me?" Addie sputtered. "Whose idea was it to chase after this guy in the first place?!"

"Who said they knew about a path that led to the main road!?" he retorted. "Leave it to a girl to get lost in her own back yard." He shook his head. "How come girls never know anything about where they live?"

"Maybe I don't because I haven't lived here much longer than you have."

"What?"

"We just moved here in May," Addie said. "I haven't had a chance to get out and explore. Especially on the property of an old lady who's supposed to be weird."

"Well, I guess it doesn't make any difference now. We're lost, no matter whose fault it is." He leaned against a tree, and Addie sat down on a stump beside him.

Out of the blue, he asked, "Is your dad really a minister?"

She nodded.

"Don't you hate it?"

"No! Why should I hate it?"

"You know, having to be good all the time. Never having any fun."

"What makes you think I don't have any fun? Look at me now," she said. "I'm having a blast."

"Yeah, right." Then he asked, "What kind of a preacher is he?"

"What do you mean?"

"You know, is he a Methodist or a Catholic or . . ."

Addie burst out laughing. "Well, he's not a Catholic, that's for sure." Nicholas looked confused.

"Priests don't usually have kids," she said with a grin.

"Oh, yeah." Nicholas blushed bright red.

"Anyway, to answer your question," Addie said, "he's not anything right now. He's not working as a minister."

"Why not?"

"He's the manager of a Christian radio station."

"Why did he quit being a preacher?"

"Because," she said impatiently, "he took this job at the radio station. He prayed about it and decided that's where God wanted him."

"Oh." Nicholas looked bored with the conversation. He glanced at Addie's watch. "What time is it?"

"About 3:30," she answered. Only 3:30. The movie this afternoon had ended at 2:30. Now, an hour later, she was sitting next to a boy she had known for less than an hour. So far he had bullied her, tried to talk her into breaking into someone's house, and led her into this menacing forest chasing a complete (and probably dangerous) stranger. What else could happen?

CHAPTER 4

The Blue Car

They sat in silence for several minutes, then Addie stood up. "Well, I'm not going to stay here," she said. "We can go back the way we came, or we can go ahead and see where it takes us. I vote for going ahead."

Nicholas stood up and nodded. "I'm with you. Maybe we're closer—" He was interrupted by the sound of a car door, then a motor roaring to life.

"Hurray!" he shouted. They began tearing through the woods toward the sound of the noise. One hundred yards later they were out of the trees and standing on the main road, just in time to see a dark blue Ford turn the corner that led back to Miss Tisdale's house.

"We missed him!" Nicholas stamped his foot and kicked a smashed pop can into the ditch across the road. "Wouldn't you know it."

"Maybe not," Addie said. "He's headed back to the mansion. I wonder what he plans on doing?"

Nicholas looked confused. "That's the way back to the mansion? Boy, am I mixed up."

"I know," she answered. "That path must have wound around a dozen times. We spent 20 minutes in those woods and it will only take us about five to get back to Miss Tisdale's."

"Do you think we can get our bikes without her seeing us?" Nick asked.

"Probably not," Addie said. "We can try. Let's go."

They hiked down the main road to the corner. It was only about a half-mile to Miss Tisdale's house. A few minutes later Addie was peering over the hedge for the second time that afternoon. There was no sign of a dark blue Ford. And no sign of their bikes.

"Great." Nicholas began stamping and kicking again.

"Cool it, would you?" Addie was getting a little disgusted with Nicholas and his quick temper. "Miss Tisdale probably took them around back. We'll have to ask her."

Addie led the way to the back door. The bikes were there, leaning against the side of the house. The two of them looked at each other silently, each thinking the same thing. Should they try to get them without being seen?

The question was answered for them before they had time to speak. Miss Tisdale opened the back door to set out her garbage and spotted them. She pursed her lips as she came down the steps and Addie braced herself. Nicholas spoke before Miss Tisdale had the chance.

"Thanks for getting our bikes," he said. "You never know who you can trust around here."

"What?" Miss Tisdale cupped her hand behind her ear and Nicholas raised his voice.

"I said, you never know who you—"

"I certainly thought I could trust you two, but you turned out to be like all the rest!" She interrupted him and Nicholas looked genuinely surprised. "Don't play innocent with me, Mr. Brady. I saw you sneaking around the house and back into the woods. Why didn't you ask me if you could play in there? Did you think I would say no?"

"We didn't think . . ." Nicholas began, but Miss Tisdale continued to talk as if she didn't hear him.

"Well, you would have been right. I don't let anyone play in there. It's much too easy to get lost. The only path winds around and the brush is so thick everywhere else it's like trying to fight your way through a jungle."

"I guess we didn't think about what we were doing," Nicholas said and Miss Tisdale relented a bit.

"I don't know what I would have done if you had gotten lost," she fretted, more worried than angry.

"We're sorry, Miss Tisdale," Addie said. "We won't go in there again."

"Well . . ." she studied their sweat-streaked faces for a few seconds, then her frown faded and she almost smiled. Addie noticed for the first time what bright blue eyes she had behind her bifocals. "All right," she said. "Go on home. You both look like you could use a bath. And don't think you can pull too much over on me," she continued. Her finger wagged right under Nicholas' nose and Addie giggled. "I'm pretty quick. That goes for you too, miss." She turned on Addie, and the young girl choked back another laugh. "If you're going to come visit me, you'll have to obey my rules."

"Yes, ma'am," Nicholas and Addie mumbled in unison. They started down the drive and Addie turned to say goodbye.

"We'll see you soon," she said.

"What?"

Addie just smiled and waved. The old woman waved back, picked up the garbage can she had just brought out, and carried it back inside.

Nicholas spoke. "Does she always carry her garbage in and out of the house?" The screen door banged open and Miss Tisdale carried the can back down the steps and set it in the grass.

"You silly children got me so worried I forgot what I was doing." She looked up to see them watching her and frowned. "Go on, now, get out of here. You've caused me enough trouble for one day." She shooed them down the driveway and went inside.

They were silent as they stood at the edge of the road, waiting for a car to pass. Addie finally spoke.

"I feel like we've already broken a rule."

"Why?" Nick asked.

"Because we didn't tell her about seeing the man in her attic. I still don't think she knew he was there."

"Well, he's gone now," Nicholas said. "I don't think he'll come back." He paused. "Do you? Do you think she's in danger?"

"No," Addie said. "When he looked at me through the window, I didn't get the feeling he was dangerous. Just . . . sneaky."

They mounted their bikes and pedaled slowly down the road toward Nicholas' house. "I hope she's okay." Nicholas said. "I like her a lot."

"Me, too. She reminds me of my grandma. Kind of fussy and forgetful, but real nice. I think I'll check on her tomorrow. Just in case."

"I'll go with you," Nicholas said. "Whatever made you think she was weird, anyway? She's not weird at all. Maybe a little rough on the outside, but real soft on the inside."

Addie nodded. "I think she's lonely, too. No matter what she says about liking her privacy."

"Well, now she's got us." Nicholas grinned as they approached his house. "See you tomorrow." He slowed down to pull into his driveway.

"Bye, Nicholas," Addie called over her shoulder.

"Nick," he shouted after her. "Nobody calls me Nicholas. Just Nick."

"Okay," she yelled back. Nick Brady. She said the name to herself several times and decided she liked it. She liked him, too. Maybe the summer wasn't going to be so bad after all.

After that, Nick and Addie were together nearly every day. It seemed strange to Addie, being friends with a boy. All her friends in Wisconsin had been girls. She could tell it was strange for Nick, too. At first he acted as if it were an honor for Addie, a lowly girl, to be allowed to tag along with a macho kid like him. But when he discovered she could run as fast as he could, climb trees better, and throw a pretty mean curve ball, he came down off his pedestal. Then they began to have fun.

They spent a lot of time exploring the country around the four-mile square. Most of it was corn and bean fields, but their favorite spot was a creek that ran under the main road north of Nick's house. It wasn't visible from the road; you had to go down a steep embankment to get to it. The creek was shallow and sparkly and lined with trees. It was a perfect place for two kids to play—close to home, but very private.

Another favorite place was Miss Tisdale's. They visited "Miss T." almost every day, and there were always cookies to eat. She even gave them a tour of her mansion.

The huge old house was in a sad state of disrepair, but there was still a whisper of the grace and charm it must have held many years ago. The rooms were large and square with big pocket doors. Solid oak woodwork framed all the windows, and there were intricately carved baseboards throughout the house. Old-fashioned wallpaper—a different style in every room—was beginning to droop from the ceilings and its seams were yellow with age. A crystal chandelier hung in the formal dining room. An immense marble fireplace with an oak mantel filled one wall and an open staircase graced another.

The second floor rooms were even larger, with walk-in closets and floor to ceiling windows. Each room had its own balcony and the master bedroom had a smaller version of the dining room fireplace. The whole house was sparsely furnished and any noise seemed to echo in the near-empty rooms.

When the children asked to see the attic, Miss T. ended the tour. "No," she said, "my attic is no different than anyone else's. It's big and messy and very dusty. Nothing much to see up there."

So they satisfied themselves with playing out in the empty greenhouse whenever they had the chance. They spent one whole morning convincing Miss T. it was a perfectly safe place to play. She finally relented and for a week, Nick and Addie kept themselves occupied trying to solve the mystery of the "Stranger in the Attic." Addie decided if they were going to solve a mystery, they should give it a name. Nick agreed.

"Sounds like a good name for a movie," he said.

"Alfred Hitchcock once made a movie named 'Stranger on a Train,'" Addie admitted. "That's where I got the idea."

"I didn't think you came up with it all by yourself," he grinned. "How do you know so much about old movies?"

"My dad loves 'em. He majored in film when he was in college," Addie explained.

"I thought he was a preacher." Nick sounded confused.

"He is—was—is—" Addie stopped and started over. "He got an undergraduate degree in film, then went on to seminary."

Nick shook his head. "Strange combination."

"I guess it is," Addie laughed. "Dad became a Christian his last year of college. He still loved film, but he realized he wanted to do something more worthwhile with his life. So he went to sem. Seminary," she added at Nick's confused look.

"More worthwhile?" he sputtered. "There's big bucks in movies!"

"But no real eternal value." Addie echoed her father's words.

Nick just shook his head and changed subjects abruptly. "So what's the scenario for today?"

"You go first," Addie said. "I went first yesterday." Each day, they both made up their own version of who the mystery man could be. Then they took a vote to see which idea was the best. Going first was a definite disadvantage. If you couldn't come up with a very good story, it was easy for the other person to take a little bit of what you had said and make up a story that was better than yours.

"I think . . ." Nick dragged out his words, stalling for time, so Addie kicked his tennis shoe. "Okay, okay," he said. "I think he's a fugitive from the law—probably a murderer or a robber or something—and he's holed up in Miss T.'s attic until the heat's off. He just goes out every once in a while to get food and stuff."

Addie rolled her eyes. "How dumb can you get?" she asked. "Robbers and murderers don't wear expensive raincoats and drive nice cars."

"They do if they're rich robbers and murderers," he grinned.

"If they're rich, they don't have to rob or murder." Nick threw some dirt at her. "I think," Addie said, "he's Miss T.'s long lost son. He's—" She raised her voice to drown out Nick's shouts of laughter. "He's also a murderer, and he's come back to his mother, hoping she'll take him in and protect him. But he's afraid to tell her what he's done, now that he's seen her, because he doesn't want to do anything that will endanger her delicate health."

Nick laughed even louder. "Miss T. is as healthy as a horse. She could probably beat up both our fathers." He stopped laughing abruptly as the sound of angry voices drifted back from the house.

The two children raced out into the yard. There, sitting in the driveway, was a dark blue car.

Addie grabbed Nick's arm and shook it furiously. "He's back, Nick! Why didn't we say anything? What should we do?"

Nick shook his head and held a finger to his lips. "Listen."

Miss T.'s voice carried clearly out the back door and she sounded angrier than the children had ever heard her.

"I won't let you do this to me! I won't!"

CHAPTER 5

Francine

"Come on!" Nick's frantic whisper jolted Addie into motion and they ran for the kitchen window. Kneeling beneath it, they listened as another voice interrupted Miss T.

"Aunt Eunice, I'm only thinking of your welfare. You're just too old to stay here by yourself any longer. Every time I visit I'm afraid to leave for fear something will happen to you."

Addie peeked over the ledge. A tall, thin, middle-aged woman with short dark hair stood by the sink, her hands on her hips. She was scowling at Miss T. and Miss T. was scowling back. There was an uncanny resemblance between the two that made Addie feel she was looking at Miss T. today and 30 years ago.

She slipped back to the ground. "It's not the mystery man," she breathed into Nick's ear. Giving the car a closer look, she saw that this one was a Chevy, not a Ford, and the color of blue wasn't even the same.

"And just what do you think is going to happen to me, Francine?" Miss T.'s voice was so sharp it could have cut paper. Addie and Nick looked at one another knowingly. They had heard that tone of voice often enough to know it meant trouble for whoever was on the receiving end.

"What if you fell and hurt yourself? You know Willard's mother sprained her ankle just last week."

"Willard's mother is even less coordinated than Willard, if that's possible. She could trip over a crack in the sidewalk. Besides, you're a fine one to talk. Who went flying down the aisle at the super-market last week and knocked over a whole display of pantyhose?"

Francine began to sputter and Nick's shoulders shook with laughter. Addie dug her elbow into his ribs and put a finger to her lips.

"Things like that happen to everyone," Francine snapped.

"Yes, Francine, things like that happen to every-one, regardless of their age."

"Aunt Eunice, when are you going to face the fact that you're getting old?"

There was a long pause. When Miss T. spoke, her voice had lost all its anger. "Francine, I think if you had your way, you'd wrap me in a blanket and park me in a wheelchair all day long. I might not get around the way I used to, but I'm not ready for that."

Francine relented. "I'm sorry, Aunt Eunice, but I worry. Especially now that your hearing has gotten so bad. You need a hearing aid. Did you talk to your doctor about that yet?"

"Yes." Miss T. sighed loudly. "I mean, I think so. I forget."

"And that's another thing," Francine persisted. "I tell you to do something and you say you forget. I don't know if you really forget or if you're just being stubborn. Either way, you need someone to help you with things like that. If you were in a retirement home . . ."

"No!" Miss T. spit out the word. "I will not even consider it." Addie peered over the ledge once more and saw the look of determination on the old woman's face. Miss T. could be stubborn. So could Francine.

"Well, you had better consider this. You can't afford to stay in this rundown old house much longer. Doug and Tim are going to be in college in a few years and we can't afford to support them and you."

"You don't support me!" Miss T. snapped and Francine backed down just a little.

"I know, I know," she said. "But your savings won't cover all your expenses much longer. At least your insurance would help pay for a retirement home." She paused. "I know you don't like to talk about this, Aunt Eunice, but won't you please reconsider selling some of your . . ."

"Francine, that's enough. We have had this conversation before and I refuse to have it again. The answer is still no."

"I'm only trying to help," Francine said with a sniff. "If you don't want my help, that's fine. But I think your attic is a silly place to hide those priceless old—"

"Francine, it's time you left." Miss T. cut her off in mid-sentence and Nick and Addie looked at each other in frustration. "I need to take a nap, now," she continued. "You know how us old people are."

"Ohhhhh," Francine practically growled at Miss T. as she walked across the kitchen to the back door. Addie and Nick scrambled to get around the corner of the house before the screen opened. Francine stomped down the steps and into her car. She revved the motor and sprayed gravel into the yard as she peeled down the driveway in reverse.

Nick clutched his hair with both hands and spoke through gritted teeth. "I don't believe this! We were so close to finding out what's in the attic. What could it be?"

"I don't know," Addie answered, "but whatever it is, it probably explains why the mystery man was here."

Nick asked what they were both thinking. "How can we get up there?"

"We can't, Nick. You know that. She made the attic off limits from the beginning. We couldn't even sneak up there. She watches us like a hawk whenever we're inside."

"Yeah, you're right," he sighed. "If we only knew what was there, maybe we could figure out a way to get Miss T. to sell it. It sounds like that's the only way she's going to get to stay here. Francine's ready to kick her out on the street. You don't want her to go to a retirement home, do you?"

"Of course not," Addie said. "But I don't know what we can do about it." She snapped her fingers. "I've got it. Now is the time to tell her we saw a man in the attic the first day we were here. If she knows we saw someone upstairs, she might be willing to tell us what's there that's so valuable."

"Good thinking," Nick answered. "Let's do it."

They ran up the steps to the back door and Nick pressed his face into the screen. "Hey, Miss T.!" he called. "Can we come in?" There was no answer, so he yelled again at the top of his lungs. "Miss T.!"

There were footsteps in the living room and Miss T. appeared. She blew her nose hard as she walked over to the screen door. "Good Lord, child," she grumbled, "I'm not that deaf."

"Don't use the Lord's name in vain," Addie said automatically and then clamped her mouth shut. Miss T. and Nick both looked at her in surprise. "I mean, it's disrespectful," she said lamely. "My dad says it's wrong to use His name that way, even if you're angry or upset. He wouldn't use yours like that."

Nick just shook his head and Miss T. sniffed, so Addie changed the subject. "We thought we'd come tell you goodbye before we went home."

"Yeah," Nick joined in. "And we wanted to ask you something." He paused and looked to Addie for help.

"We saw that lady leave just now. Is she a relative of yours?" Addie asked.

"My niece," Miss T. snapped.

"Oh. Do you have any nephews?" Addie ignored Miss T.'s obvious desire to squelch any more questions.

"Not a blessed one, thank Go– thank heaven. Can I thank heaven?" she asked crossly.

"Sure," Addie smiled. "Then who was that man we saw the day we met you?" She tried to sound as if it was a perfectly natural thing to ask.

"What man?" Miss T. glanced from Addie to Nick and back to Addie. "When did you ever see a man here?"

"Oh, it wasn't Mr. Crenshaw," Nick assured her. "This was a young guy. Kind of young, I mean. Younger than you, anyway."

"Everybody's younger than me," Miss T. retorted.

"We just saw him wandering around, and thought you must know him," Addie said.

"I wasn't aware there was anyone wandering 'around' as you put it. Just where is 'around'?" Miss T. bent over to look Addie square in the eye. "Come on, miss. Be honest. Where was he?"

Addie swallowed. "In the attic," she answered and held her breath.

Miss T. backed slowly to the table, pulled out a chair and sat down. Her face was white and her jaws were clenched. Addie went to her and put a hand on her shoulder. "Don't worry, Miss T. We haven't seen him since. I don't think he meant any harm. We can call the sheriff if you want to, though."

At the mention of a sheriff, Miss T.'s back straightened and her eyes snapped. "No!" The word exploded into the quiet kitchen and Nick and Addie jumped. "That man is none of your business. I don't ever want you to mention him to me—or to anyone else—again. Do you understand me?"

CHAPTER 6

The Forgotten Appointment

"Do you understand?" she repeated and Addie nodded. Miss T. looked at Nick.

"Sure, sure, anything you say." His head bobbed up and down and Miss T. seemed satisfied. Her customary frown slowly replaced the stunned anger on her face and she looked at both children with obvious disgust.

"You're filthy," she exlaimed. "How did I ever let you talk me into allowing you to play in that dirty old greenhouse in the first place? I don't think—"

"But it isn't that dirty—"

"You can't make us quit—"

Addie and Nick stumbled over each other's words in their haste to stop Miss T. She clapped her hands sharply and they stuttered to a stop.

"It is that dirty and I can make you do anything I want. It's my property." She paused. "And what I think I will do is require that you help me clean the greenhouse thoroughly before you play in it again." Something close to a smile crossed her face as Nick and Addie sighed with relief. "Tomorrow. Eight o'clock. Don't be late."

"We won't be," Addie assured her. They clattered out the back door and took their bikes from their customary parking spot against the house.

"See you then," Addie called. Miss T. waved at them absentmindedly from the window. Nick mounted his bike and zoomed down the drive so fast Addie had a hard time keeping up with him.

"What's your rush?" she called, but he just motioned her on and kept riding. She hadn't caught up with him when he braked to a stop at the corner. His excited chatter started before she reached him.

"Do you believe it?" he exclaimed. "Miss T. must be into something big! That sly old fox. She sure had us fooled. And to think we felt sorry for her!"

"Into what, Nick? You're not making any sense."

"Okay, pea-brain, I'll say this slowly so you can understand. Miss T. knows all about the man in her attic. Whatever he's doing must be part of a plan they've thought of together. Why else would she want us to keep quiet about it? Francine knows there's something valuable there, and she wants Miss T. to sell it. Miss T. refuses. That doesn't make any sense, since she's in danger of losing everything. Unless," he paused for dramatic effect, "unless she's holding out because the mystery man can do something more for her. Maybe her stuff is real valuable on the black market."

"What's the black market?"

"I'm not sure, but I know it's illegal," he answered. "Or maybe," now he was getting really excited, "maybe the guy is blackmailing her because he knows something about her past that would ruin her reputation."

"Miss T. doesn't give a rip about her reputation and you know it," Addie interrupted and Nick faltered just a little. "Put your brain in gear before your mouth gets moving, would you?"

Addie continued. "I agree, Miss T. does know something about the man, but not because she's in on any bizarre plan with him."

"Then what?"

Addie opened and shut her mouth a couple of times, hoping a snappy answer would come. It didn't. "I don't know. I just know she's too honest to be involved in something shady."

Addie mounted her bike again and continued down the road. Nick circled around her as she thought. Finally she spoke. "All we can do is go to help her clean tomorrow and find out whatever we can."

"Well, of course that's what we're going to do," he said. "What did you think, I was going to write 'The End' and roll the credits for 'The Stranger in the Attic'?" His voice dropped to a theatrical whisper and Addie stuck her tongue out at him.

"See you tomorrow, spoilsport," he shouted and pulled a wheelie in his driveway as Addie pedaled on.

She swerved to the other side of the road when she got close to home. The farmer who owned the field next to her house had double-cropped this year and the irrigation system that watered the newly-sprouting beans sprayed out into the road. She sat under the spray and was soon soaked to the skin. Her mother would have kittens, but she needed to calm down and think through what had happened today.

Addie would never believe Miss T. was part of anything crooked. Her father always said people who valued integrity in others demanded it most of themselves. Miss T. was no different. Addie knew in her heart the old woman was the victim and not the crook. Maybe tomorrow they would find out more.

Eight o'clock comes awfully early on a hot summer morning. Addie barely had time to gulp down a bite of toast and some juice before she poked her head into the family room to tell her mother goodbye. Mrs. McCormick was having her quiet time and Addie sighed. Lately she and her mother had been reading Psalms, and Addie really enjoyed it. She regretted missing their time together.

"Bye, Mom," she whispered. Mrs. McCormick looked up from her Bible and Addie could see the disappointment in her eyes.

"Where are you off to so early?" she asked.

"Miss T. wants us to help her clean out the greenhouse this morning, and we promised we'd be there by 8," Addie answered.

Her mother smiled. "You really like Miss Tisdale, don't you?"

Addie nodded. She started to speak, then changed her mind.

"What is it, hon?" her mother asked.

Addie sat down on the arm of the sofa. "Miss T. is having some problems right now."

"What kind of problems?"

"I'm not sure," Addie said. "I think she's kind of poor and her niece wants her to use her insurance to go to a home."

Her mother shook her head sympathetically. "It's always sad to see that happen to an elderly person."

"But I don't think it has to happen!" Addie sounded frustrated, and her mother looked puzzled. "She's got some valuable things she could sell, but she won't and we—"

"Addie," her mother interrupted and there was a hint of warning in her voice. "Are you butting in somewhere you shouldn't be?"

"But Mom, if we could only convince her . . ."

"Addie." Her mother spoke sternly and the young girl quieted. "We've talked about this before. I know you only want to help, but you can't run other people's lives. If you really want to help Miss T., pray for her. The Lord will show you if there's anything else you can do."

Addie sighed. "Okay, Mom."

Nick was waiting for her at the edge of his drive. "I almost left without you," he stormed. "We've got about two minutes to get there, Addie. What were you doing, saying your prayers?" Nick had walked in on Addie and her mom reading the Bible one morning and had teased her about it ever since.

"Yeah, I was praying for you," she retorted. She meant it as a joke, but Nick gave her a strange look.

"Really?"

"Well..." she could tell his question was a serious one, so she hedged around the truth. "I have prayed for you before."

"Why?" he asked.

"Lord, forgive me," she prayed, *"but it's just not the time."* She didn't think she could do justice to an explanation of why he needed Jesus in his life in the minute or two it would take them to reach Miss T.'s house, so she said simply, "I pray for all my friends."

The look on his face told Addie he didn't know if he should be flattered or offended, and she almost giggled. If she ever got the nerve to tell him about Jesus, she could see it was going to be an interesting conversation.

Miss T. was already in the greenhouse when they arrived, a bright red handkerchief tied around her head. She had on blue and white checkered pedal-pushers and a dingy white blouse. One hand held a large sponge and the other, a bucket full of warm, soapy water.

"Addie, you start on the windows," she said without even a hello. "Nick, I've got some things that need to be thrown out. You can help me carry them outside."

Addie took the sponge and turned around. A wall of grimy windows she'd never really seen before stared back at her. Nick followed Miss T. to the far end of the greenhouse, but not before he had hissed in Addie's ear, "I don't do windows." She flicked a spongeful of suds at him and started to work.

Addie's fingers were a mass of pruny wrinkles before she was even close to finished, but she decided she'd gotten the better job when she listened to Miss T. order Nick in and out of the greenhouse with a variety of objects, all dirty and all odd shapes and sizes that made them hard to carry. Pots of all kinds had to be sorted into piles that determined if they would be kept and stored or thrown out. Odd little statues with flowers in their hands and wreaths on their heads were stacked by the back door.

Addie was on the final row of windows when she heard the phone ring. Miss T. kept pulling at the heavy cast iron fence that leaned against the back wall.

"Miss T.," she called out. "Telephone."

The old woman looked up and frowned. "What?"

"Telephone," Addie yelled again.

"Oh, all right," the old woman muttered under her breath. She wiped her hands on her white blouse and hurried indoors.

Nick watched her disappear through the back door and then he collapsed. His face was almost muddy from the combination of sweat and dirt. Addie could hear him mumbling to himself as he used an old burlap sack to wipe his forehead. "Let me do windows. Please let me do windows."

"Serves you right," she smirked. "At least your hands don't look like dried fruit."

"Do you know how many times I've carried those pots in and out of this greenhouse?" He didn't wait for an answer. "Three times, that's how many. At first she wanted to save them to repot some ferns Francine gave her. But she remembered she threw the ferns out after they died in the heat last week, so I carried them out. Then she decided she'd break them up and use them for drainage in some larger pots she has, so I carried them back in. But she only needed a few for that, so I carried the rest back out a second time. Then she remembered she promised to save Francine any extra she had, so I brought them back in. I think she remembered what Francine said yesterday, because then she got mad all of a sudden and said if Francine needed any pots she could buy them herself."

Addie laughed as Nick rambled on about the pots, imitating Miss T.'s sharp voice.

"Come on, Nick, give her a break," she finally said. "Old people have a hard time remembering things. They can't help it."

"Then I'll let you carry them out next time and I'll finish washing windows, okay?"

"Forget it." Addie smiled at him. "You don't do windows, remember?"

"You know," he continued, "we haven't had any luck getting her to tell us about the stranger. How do we make her slow down long enough to ask her some questions?"

"Maybe we could get a cookie and something to drink," Addie answered. "She can't expect us to work all morning without a break. There *are* child labor laws."

"Good idea," he agreed. "I'm starved, anyway."

"Just don't forget the purpose of the break and spend the whole time stuffing your face."

"Me?" he hooted. "You're the one who licked the crumbs out of the bottom of the jar the other day!"

"I did not!"

"Stop arguing, both of you!" Miss T.'s sharp voice interrupted them. Addie made a face at Nick before giving her a big smile. "Say, Miss T., could we take a break?" She stopped when she saw the anger flashing in the old woman's eyes. "What's the matter?"

"We'll have to quit for the day," Miss T. snapped. "It seems I have an appointment at the doctor's."

"I thought you forgot to call . . ." Nick began, but Addie cut him short. They weren't supposed to know about that, since it was part of the conversation they had eavesdropped on the day before!

"What doctor is that?" Addie asked.

"An ear doctor," Miss T. answered. "I made the appointment and forgot all about it. That was Willard. Francine is on her way to pick me up. The doctor's office called her. They tried to reach me, but I didn't answer the phone." She pounded her fist against the doorsill. "They can't expect me to sit in the kitchen all day waiting for the phone to ring, can they? I've got better things to do." She sighed. "Of course, if I hadn't forgotten it in the first place, none of this would have happened." She bit her lip and shook her head.

"We all forget things, Miss T.," Nick said. "I forgot my mom's birthday once."

"What?" she said, not really paying attention, her eyes misty.

"I said—" Nick looked at Addie and sighed. "I said, we all forget things."

"If you forget them when you're young, they call you careless. If you forget them when you're old, they call you senile." Her shoulders sagged and she lowered herself into the iron chair that sat by the door. "Oh, children, am I really so old?"

"I think you're . . . you're one of the nicest people I know, and age doesn't have anything to do with that!" Addie's voice quivered and Miss T. smiled at her.

"Thank you, dear," she said and ruffled the girl's hair.

They watched Francine pull into the driveway and stop. She got out of the car and walked to where Miss T. sat in the door of the greenhouse. The expression on her face was a mixture of exasperation and pity. Miss T. stood to face her, and Addie was struck again by the resemblance between the two women. Until Francine opened her mouth.

"Aunt Eunice," she began in her whiny voice.

"I know, I know," Miss T. stopped her. "I'll be ready in two minutes. Children, pick up a little more in here and then go home, all right?"

She went into the house without waiting for an answer and Francine followed her.

Nick and Addie finished cleaning and left. The sky began to cloud over, and flashes of lightning lit up the southwest. Thunder rumbled in the distance and the day turned dark and dreary.

CHAPTER 7

Meeting Malcolm

The next day was no better. Rain pattered on the ground, and dark clouds filled the sky. An occasional flash of lightning showed through Addie's window and she lay in bed a long time, watching thunderheads roll across the sky. When she finally dragged herself downstairs, she found her father in the kitchen, whistling something disgustingly cheerful.

"What are you doing home?" she asked. "I thought you had an interview this morning."

"I do." He grinned. "But not until 10. I'm interviewing a 'star.'" He exaggerated the last word and Addie laughed.

"'Is he a real staaar?'" She mimicked a line from one of her father's favorite movies and he nodded his approval.

"You're getting good, kid. The star is Malcolm Griffith, a linebacker for the L.A. Raiders. He's only in town until early this afternoon, so we had to work around his schedule."

"Can I listen to the interview?" Addie loved football. Even though she didn't follow the Raiders, meeting a linebacker for a professional team would definitely be exciting.

Mr. McCormick studied her eager face. "Can you get dressed and eat your breakfast in 15 minutes?"

Addie didn't bother to answer. She dashed back upstairs and into the bathroom for a quick shower. She had her best jeans and tee-shirt on in five minutes. Her mother was putting two slices of bread in the toaster as she flew back down the stairs.

"Slow down," Mrs. McCormick said. "You have time to run a brush through your hair and eat something before you go."

Addie popped the bread out of the toaster half-done.

"I said 'eat' Addie, not inhale," her mother warned.

Addie made a small effort to look like she was slowing down. Her father walked into the kitchen from the living room and handed her a brush.

"John, not at the table," her mother protested.

"Whoops." He snatched the brush back and gave Addie a, "She's the boss," look. Addie buttered the second piece of toast and gulped it down with a glass of orange juice. She grabbed the brush from her father's hand and took three swipes down the back of her head, one down each side.

Mr. McCormick laughed. "Twelve minutes. That's got to be a record."

Mrs. McCormick sat at the table, shaking her head, and Addie gave her a quick kiss. "See you later, Mom."

There was a knock at the back door and Nick stuck his head in. "Hi, Addie. Good morning, Mrs. McCormick."

"Hi, Nick," Addie said. "Come in for a minute. Have you ever met my dad?"

Nick shook his head. "How do you do, Reverend McCormick?"

Her father smiled. "Nice to meet you, Nick. Don't bother with the reverend, okay? Even when I was a bonafide preacher, people never called me that. I prefer just plain old John."

Nick looked decidedly uncomfortable at the prospect of calling Addie's father "plain old John," so the man added, "Or Mr. McCormick, if you prefer that."

Nick nodded. "Okay, Mr. McCormick." He paused. "I thought Addie might want to go for a bike ride."

"In the rain?" Addie peered through the screen. The rain had stopped although there was still a light mist in the air. She shook her head. "I can't, Nick. I'm going with Dad to the radio station to listen to an interview he's doing this morning. Malcolm Griffith is in town." She said this as casually as she could, hoping it would get some kind of response from Nick. It did.

"Malcolm Griffith!?" His eyes grew wide and he looked at Mr. McCormick with renewed interest.

"How come you're interviewing him? He's a linebacker for the Raiders. Why would he be on a *religious* program?"

Mr. McCormick smiled at the surprise in Nick's voice and said, "Malcolm Griffith is a Christian, Nick. He's going to tell us how he came to know the Lord and what God's been doing in pro football in the last few years."

"He's a Christian?" The word came out in a squeak.

"What, did you think only wimps can be Christians?" Addie began, but her father gave her shoulder a tiny squeeze.

"Would you like to come with us and meet him, Nick?" Mr. McCormick asked.

"Sure!" Nick's grin split his face and he headed for the door. Then he stopped and turned around, his face a bright red. "Now, right?" he asked in a small voice.

Mr. McCormick laughed. "Yep, right now. Let's go."

They stopped by Nick's house first to make sure it was okay with his mom. The 30-minute ride passed quickly and both children bounded into the station, eager to meet Malcolm Griffith.

The man who rose from his chair in Mr. McCormick's office stopped Addie in her tracks. Nick bumped into her with a grunt, then backed up and was quiet.

Malcolm Griffith was the largest man Addie had ever seen. His shoulders seemed to fill the window behind him and the hand he extended in greeting dwarfed Mr. McCormick's own fairly large hand.

"It's nice to meet you, Malcolm. I'm John McCormick and this is my daughter Addie and her friend Nick." He gestured toward the children, then laughed at the expression on their faces. "Relax, kids, I think he's safe."

Malcolm took Addie's hand gently in his own. His smile was so warm Addie relaxed immediately.

"It's nice to meet you, Addie, Nick," he said. "Are you going to listen to the interview?"

"We wouldn't miss it!" Nick said fervently.

"Speaking of the interview," Mr. McCormick said, "I think we'd better get started. I know you're on a pretty tight schedule, Malcolm."

Malcolm nodded. "I'll be traveling all around central Illinois for the next two days, speaking at a couple of rallys and giving more interviews like this one."

"Kids," Mr. McCormick said, "you can't come in the taping room, but I'll turn on the intercom system so you can hear the interview outside, okay?"

The two children followed the men down the hall and settled themselves in the small waiting room. After several minutes of testing and adjusting the sound system, the interview began.

"First of all, Malcolm, I think our listeners would like to hear how you came to know the Lord," Mr. McCormick said.

"I hope I don't disappoint them. I never had one of those 'God dragged me from a bottomless pit' conversion experiences. I was raised by Christian parents and I've been a Christian a long time."

"That's really the best way, isn't it?" Mr. McCormick asked.

"Definitely. My parents gave me the faith and security I needed to make it in such a competitive sport."

"How did you come to be in football?"

"I've loved football all my life, and I think I knew early on I wanted to play. Obviously I've got the size. God gave me the talent as well. I received a scholarship to the University of Illinois straight out of high school, and did my undergraduate work there. The Lord has really opened doors for me all through the years."

"Do people ever question you about being a Christian in a game many consider violent?"

Malcolm nodded. "All the time. But there are a lot of Christians in the sport and I think most of them feel the way I do. I'm there to do the best I can. I'm out to win, but I don't have to break bones or draw blood to do the job. I'd like to think I'm blooming where I was planted. After all, I am 6-foot-4-inches and weigh 250 pounds. Combine that with my abilities and love for the sport, and it just seems natural."

The interview went on for almost an hour and Nick nudged Addie, pointing at the clock.

She nodded. "It won't be this long when Dad puts it on the air," she said. "He'll edit it down to about half an hour. He takes out the mistakes and makes it sound more polished than it does now."

When the interview ended, Malcolm came back into the waiting room and shook hands with the children once more.

"It was nice meeting you," he said. "And thank you, John. I don't normally enjoy talking with people in the media, but when they're Christians, it makes a big difference."

"What kind of a difference?" Nick asked.

Malcolm studied the boy's face and took a few seconds to answer. "Well, Nick," he said, "people in radio or television only to make money are sometimes hard to deal with. In order to get the biggest audience, they have to get a news story first, or find out something about a man no one else knows. They can twist your words to make it sound like you said something you didn't, or they invade your privacy or the privacy of your family and friends. Those kind of tactics can make a person miserable. But when I've worked with Christian people in the media, they go out of their way to make sure they get the true story about you and they respect your rights as an individual. They look at you as a person, not just a story. Do you understand what I mean?"

Nick nodded.

"Good." Malcolm smiled and glanced at his watch. "I'd better be going. My ride is probably here and I've got to get ready for the rally tonight. Are any of you coming?"

Addie and Nick both looked at Mr. McCormick with hopeful faces and he smiled. "We might," he answered. "I'll have to talk it over with Gwen—my wife—first. Where are you staying, Malcolm? Are you sure we can't give you a lift?"

Malcolm shook his head. "Thanks anyway. I've been staying with a friend of mine, Russ Krueger. He read in the paper that I'd be in the area, so he contacted me before I left Los Angeles and offered me room and board for a few days. He owns an antique store in Peoria. As far as I can tell, it's so successful he hires people to run it while he roams around the country looking for antiques. He took a few days off to play chauffeur for me though."

"That's nice," Mr. McCormick said. "It always helps to have fellowship on trips like these."

"Oh, he's not a Christian," Malcolm answered. "But we've had several talks, and I'm praying for him, so I know the Lord's working."

"What's he mean by that?" Nick whispered in Addie's ear. "Are you praying for me like that?" His eyes were anxious, and Addie was at a loss for words.

Just then, a dark blue car pulled into the parking lot and Malcolm waved to the man behind the wheel. He turned to Mr. McCormick and shook hands one last time.

"Thanks again, John. This has been a very enjoyable morning." He smiled at Addie and Nick. "Bye, kids. Hope I see you tonight."

Malcolm walked out to the waiting car and eased his massive frame into the front seat. Addie glanced at the driver and gave a soft gasp. Nick followed her gaze and his eyes widened as he watched the dark blue Ford drive away.

The mystery man had finally reappeared.

CHAPTER 8

The Rally

Addie and Nick tried to keep a normal conversation going during the ride home, but it was hard. Both of them were stunned by the revelation that the mystery man was a friend of Malcolm Griffith.

"So you think you'd like to go to the rally tonight?" Mr. McCormick asked.

"I'd love it." Nick's statement was so heartfelt Addie looked at him in surprise. He'd never responded to the one offer she'd made to take him to church, and he always avoided talking about anything related to the Lord. Addie suspected he didn't know what he was getting into.

"Well, I'm sure it will be all right with Gwen, so check with your parents. If it's okay, we'll pick you up around 6:15," Mr. McCormick said as they pulled into Nick's driveway.

"That'll be great," Nick answered. "I've never been to a rally for a pro football player before."

"That's not exactly the kind of rally we're going to, Nick," Mr. McCormick said. "Tonight there will be some music—Christian music—and some testimonies and Malcolm will give a, well, not a sermon, but something like that. Do you still want to go?"

Nick's look of enthusiasm changed to one of guarded politeness. "Will he talk about football at all?" he asked.

"Oh, I'm sure he will," Mr. McCormick laughed.

"Will there be any other kids there?" Nick was still suspicious.

"Sure," Addie said. "Lots. Everybody brings their friends to these. I bet Malcolm will even bring his friend, don't you think, Dad?" Addie asked the question innocently enough but Nick got the hint.

"I'm sure he will, honey," her father answered. "So you'll go then, Nick?"

"Sure," Nick answered. "6:15. I'll be ready." He opened the car door, then turned back with a look of resigned pain crossing his face. "Do I have to wear a tie?"

"If you do, you'll probably be the only person there with one on," Addie answered.

"Great. See you tonight." The door slammed shut.

Mr. McCormick reached over to ruffle Addie's hair as they drove home. "Nervous about Nick going along tonight, kiddo?"

Addie shook her head. "Not really. I've tried to talk to him about the Lord before but he always changes the subject. Maybe Malcolm can get through to him."

Her father smiled. "I hope so. God answers prayers in ways we'd never suspect, doesn't He?"

Addie nodded as she thought of the mystery man. *He certainly does.*

The parking lot was jammed that night. Mr. McCormick dropped the children off at the entrance while he and Addie's mom parked the car. Addie and Nick hurried into the large building and down the corridor to the main hall. Musicians were tuning up and men were standing by the door handing out tracts to the hundreds of people that filled the room. Nick and Addie found four seats on the aisle and sat down, staking a claim before anyone else grabbed them. Her parents came in a few minutes later. Then the lights dimmed, and the room full of noise and laughter and coughing and babies crying suddenly became quiet.

Bright pictures flashed onto three screens that hung from the high ceiling. Mostly pictures of Malcolm, they alternated between shots of him on the field or at home, with friends or at Bible study. It was an impressive multi-media presentation and when it was over, Addie glanced at Nick. He was applauding vigorously, and she relaxed.

Several local athletes gave their testimonies and another woman sang "Amazing Grace." The song was pretty off-key and Addie could tell Nick was close to laughter. She poked him in the ribs and he poked her back. Mr. McCormick leaned forward slightly and gave them "the look." They settled down and clapped loudly when the woman finished.

Then Malcolm was introduced. He stepped up to the podium and even from a distance, he looked huge. There were soft gasps all around the auditorium, mainly from women who had no idea of the size of a pro football player. Malcolm ignored the gasps and smiled.

"I'm glad to see so many of you here tonight. I want to share with you just a little of what my life is like as a Christian and as a football player. But most of all, I hope I can introduce some of you to the best friend I've ever had, Jesus Christ."

He paused, and Addie glanced at Nick. He was squirming in his chair. When he saw Addie watching him, he rolled his eyes.

Malcolm spoke for over an hour, and it was a gripping message. As he finished, the room was so still the sound of a distant siren could be heard through the open windows.

"My nephew looked at my muscles one day and said, 'You must not be afraid of anybody.'" Malcolm shook his head. "That's not true. It doesn't matter how big you are or how tough you are. There's always someone bigger and tougher. I learn that lesson in almost every game I play. Don't get me wrong. I stay in shape and I play hard on the field, but ultimately, Jesus Christ is my protection."

"Another child once asked if I make a lot of money." Malcolm paused, took a deep breath and grinned. "Yeah, I do." Laughter rippled through the crowd. "I make a *lot* of money! But I learned early on that money can't be my security. My father was in a very serious car accident my first year in pro ball and it took every penny I earned to pay the doctors that saved his life. If I had expected my salary to make my future secure, I would have been disappointed. But I didn't expect that, because I know that money is not my security. Jesus Christ is."

"Finally," he concluded, "a talk show host once asked me how it felt to be admired by millions of people." He paused. "It's nice," he admitted with another smile. "But the fans who applaud me today will say 'Malcolm who?' 10 years from now. It's only in the eyes of Jesus Christ that I have eternal value." He stopped then and his eyes searched the crowd for several seconds. "I'd like to pray now, and if there's anyone here who wants the eternal security only Jesus Christ can give, please pray this prayer with me."

As Malcolm prayed the prayer of salvation, Addie squinted at Nick through one eye. He sat on the edge of his chair and his hands were gripping it so hard his knuckles were white. His eyes were open wide and his jaw was set. Addie had seen that same stubborn look a dozen times before and she sighed. Her father reached over to pat her leg softly. At the amen, they all stood to sing the closing song.

Afterward, scores of people crowded the stage to talk to Malcolm. Addie and Nick stood to one side, and waited until most of them were gone. Nick was quieter than usual and Addie didn't try to make conversation. Malcolm looked tired but very happy as he prayed with a boy who couldn't have been much older than the two children. He smiled when he saw them waiting by the stage.

"Hi, Addie. Hi, Nick." He placed one large arm around Nick's shoulders and the other around Addie's, then hugged them gently. Addie hugged him back and even Nick grinned, a little embarrassed, but pleased. "I'm glad you came tonight," he said.

"Hey, Malcolm," someone said in a loud voice behind them. Malcolm glanced around. "I've got the car parked out back, anytime you're ready to go."

"Thanks, Russ," Malcolm answered. "I shouldn't be too much longer."

Addie froze, staring straight ahead, afraid to turn and face the mystery man. Nick had no such reservations and spun around.

"Russ, these are a couple of friends I met at the radio station today. This is Nick Brady and this young lady . . ." Malcolm forcibly turned Addie around, "this young lady is Addie McCormick. Kids, this is Russ Krueger."

Russ gave them both a friendly nod. He stood with one foot on the first step of the stage. A grey raincoat was draped casually over his left arm. It was the same raincoat he wore the day Addie saw him in the attic window. His eyes were dark brown, and they seemed to get even darker when he recognized Addie. His smile faded.

CHAPTER 9

Malcolm's Friend

"How do you do, Addie," Russ said soberly.

"How do you do," she said, her voice barely audible.

"I believe I've seen you around, haven't I?" he asked.

Addie simply nodded.

"You two know each other?" Malcolm asked.

"We were both visitors in the home of a mutual . . . acquaintance in the area," Russ answered. "Eunice Tisdale."

"Isn't she one of your business prospects, Russ?" When Russ nodded, Malcolm said, "How do you know her, Addie?"

"She's my neighbor," Addie said. "And she's really nice. She lives by herself in the country. And she likes it that way. She doesn't appreciate people bothering her and she . . ."

"You seem to know Miss Tisdale well," Russ interrupted.

"We both know her," Nick chimed in. "And we like her a lot and we'd do anything for her. *Anything*."

Russ smiled slightly at the veiled threat. "I'm sure you would, son." He turned to Malcolm. "Ready?"

"Sure," Malcolm answered. "Goodbye, kids. Take care of yourselves."

"Bye," Addie answered.

"Goodbye, Malcolm," Nick said pointedly and glared at Russ.

Russ arched an eyebrow and said softly, "Maybe I'll see you again sometime."

"Not if we see you first," Nick muttered under his breath as the two men walked away.

The ride home was quiet. Mr. McCormick pulled into Nick's driveway and Nick got out. "Thanks for asking me along, Mr. and Mrs. McCormick. See you tomorrow, Addie."

As they drove the last mile home, Mr. McCormick asked, "Do you think Malcolm made an impression on Nick tonight, Addie?"

"What? Oh, yeah, I think he did." Addie forced the picture of Russ Krueger's polite smile out of her head and tried to concentrate on more important things. "Nick's just so stubborn. If he thinks you want him to do something, he won't, even if he knows it's the right thing to do."

"Be patient with him, Addie," her mother said. "The Lord's timing might not agree with yours, but it will be perfect for Nick."

The next morning Addie and Nick met at the creek. They waded up and down the shallow bed, trying to catch minnows with their bare hands.

"I don't know, Addie," Nick said. "Maybe we're making a mountain out of a molehill." He stood perfectly still in the middle of the creek, waiting to grab several of the tiny fish that were swimming near his feet. Addie tripped on a rock and the fish darted away.

"Thanks a lot," Nick muttered. "I mean, the guy seems like a creep, but there's nothing mysterious about him," he went on. "He owns an antique shop. Miss T. has antiques. He wants them. She won't sell. Big deal. There's nothing mysterious about that."

"He shouldn't have been sneaking around Miss T.'s attic," Addie said.

"Sneaking? What makes you think he was sneaking? Miss T. knew he was there. You can't be accused of sneaking around someone's house if they know you're doing it."

"Well..." Addie searched for another thread to hang her mystery on. "Why doesn't Miss T. want to sell? That's strange, don't you think? I mean, it's that or a retirement home. Don't you think she'd be sensible enough to sell if she wasn't trying to hide something?"

"Maybe those antiques are family heirlooms. There are a lot of people who'd rather go through Chinese water torture than sell something that's been in their family for eons," Nick said.

"It can't be something in the family," Addie protested, "or Francine wouldn't want to sell it either."

"Yeah, right. Francine would sell her own grandmother if she had the chance." Nick dismissed any notion of Francine's family loyalty with a wave of his hand.

"Maybe you're right," Addie sighed. She dug her big toe into the cold sand. "Come on, let's go." She waded out of the creek and dried her feet on the grass. They scrambled up the embankment and got on their bikes.

Five minutes later they were in Miss T.'s driveway. Fresh tire tracks ran to the back of the house. Addie pointed to them silently.

Nick shrugged. "Probably Francine, back to put the screws to Miss T. about moving out."

"Maybe."

Addie pedaled slowly down the drive. She rested her bike by the side of the house, instead of around the corner like she usually did, and Nick followed her example. They walked noiselessly through the grass. Addie tried to appear casual as she stepped around the corner.

Russ Krueger stood at the back door with his nose pressed to the screen. He hadn't heard the children approach and Addie and Nick watched as he opened the screen and rattled the knob on the inside door, then tried to open it. It was locked. That told Addie and Nick Miss T. was gone (she never locked her doors when she was home), but it didn't seem to tell Russ anything. He played with the knob and pushed on the door as if that would help.

Finally, he reached into his pocket and pulled out a small knife. He inserted the blade into the old-fashioned lock and jiggled it.

"What are you doing!?" Addie practically shouted.

Russ stepped back quickly and concealed the knife in his hand. He walked slowly down the steps and Addie heard the blade click softly as he dropped it in his pocket. "I just came to pay Miss Tisdale a visit," he said with a forced smile. "After our little chat last night, I thought I'd better talk to her before you did, or she'd never let me in her house again."

"I don't think she wants you in her house now," Addie retorted. "That's why the door's locked. Or hadn't you noticed?"

"I knocked first," Russ answered smoothly. "I just assumed she didn't hear me. She does have a hearing problem. Or hadn't you noticed?" He mocked Addie gently and the girl gritted her teeth.

"What's in her attic that you want so badly?" she asked.

"If Miss Tisdale hasn't divulged that information, I don't think it's my place to tell you," Russ answered shortly. "Obviously, you don't know her as well as you claim."

"We know her well enough to know she doesn't want you slinking around her house when she's gone!" Addie said.

Nick added, "She doesn't even want you slinking around when she's here!"

"Then I will leave." Russ gave them a slight bow and walked to his car. When his back was to them,

Nick moved quickly and scooped something out of the grass by the bottom step. Then he spoke.

"Tell us what's in the attic or we'll tell the police you tried to break into Miss T.'s house."

Russ gave a short laugh. "And just how would you prove that?"

Nick opened his fist to reveal the pocket knife Russ had dropped. The man's eyes flashed angrily. "Gim'me the knife, kid," he said.

CHAPTER 10

The Fire

Nick stuffed the knife in his own pocket and said, "Tell us what's in the attic."

Russ thrust out his hand and took a step toward the young boy. Nick held his ground. They glared at one another for several seconds. Finally Russ backed off. He leaned against his car and studied his fingernails. When he looked up the anger was gone from his eyes.

"Do you *really* think I'm a criminal?" he asked.

Surprised at the question, Nick stammered, "Well, yes —I mean, why else—you were—"

Addie interrupted him. "You were trying to get into Miss T.'s house without her permission. What does that make you?"

Russ grinned. "*You've* never tried to do that, have you?" Addie swallowed hard and Nick turned bright red. "What does that make you?" he asked.

"We want to help her!"

"What makes you think I don't!?" Russ gestured to the house and yard around him. "Look at this place. It's falling apart and the inside is no better.

The old gal needs money. I could make a deal for her that . . ." he stopped. "Well, let's just say her money problems would be over."

Addie shook her head. "It's not that simple. If it were, I think she'd sell, whatever it is. There's got to be a reason she won't. Do you know what it is?"

Russ refused to meet Addie's gaze and for the first time since they met him, he seemed uncomfortable. "You don't want to know, kid."

Addie and Nick exchanged glances and a knot of fear began to churn in Addie's stomach. Maybe Miss T. *was* involved in something dishonest!

"Well," Nick said after an awkward silence, "if you want an answer to your first question, yes, I do think you're a criminal! You've already been in her attic once, and you know she doesn't want to sell whatever is up there. Why were you trying to break in today if you weren't going to rob her?"

"Ain't nothin' *in* her attic, kid. That's the problem. I'm just trying to find out where she's . . ." He broke off once more and shook his head. "I can't believe I'm telling you this. I've got better things to do." He opened the car door and stepped in.

"Russ?" Addie said.

"Yeah?"

"How did you and Malcolm get to be such good friends?"

"We grew up together, played ball in high school. After college, Malcolm went pro and I opened my store. He offered to make some contacts for me in 'high society' and I realized how valuable our friendship could be. I've kept up with him ever since."

Addie's disgust must have shown on her face, because Russ shrugged and said, "You gotta look out for number one, kid."

Addie didn't answer and Russ grinned. "Besides, I'm a lost soul. Malcolm's a sucker for lost souls. Or hadn't you noticed?" Nodding at Nick, he said, "Keep the knife, kid." The engine roared to life and he was gone.

They watched the car disappear down the road. Nick pulled the knife from his pocket and sat down on the bottom step. Addie sank down beside him.

"That was a pretty brave thing you did, Nick," she said. He shrugged. "Stupid, but brave."

"Yeah," he grinned, "I'm glad I didn't have time to think about it." His smile faded. "A lot of good it did us."

Addie voiced what they were both thinking. "What do you suppose he meant when he said we didn't want to know her reasons for not selling?"

"I'm not sure," Nick answered, "but I don't think it's anything good. Even Russ seemed upset by it."

"Yeah. And if the antiques aren't in the attic, where are they?"

"Francine thinks they're in the attic," Nick said.

"That's right!" Addie sat up straighter, thinking hard. "Do you remember what Francine said that first day? 'Your attic is a silly place to *hide* those priceless, old ___'"

"You mean Russ just couldn't find them? Miss T. has them hidden?"

"She must have!" Addie's excitement faded. "Of course, we'll never know because we'll never have the chance to get up there and look." She sighed. "So what do you think about our mystery now? Is this mysterious enough for you?"

Nick nodded. "Too mysterious." He paused. "Too serious."

They got their bikes and headed for home. Neither spoke until they turned the corner to Nick's house. "Russ is right about one thing," he said. "Malcolm must be a real sucker to stay friends with a guy who's just using him."

"I think Malcolm knows exactly what he's doing," Addie protested. "That doesn't mean he's a sucker. He's just willing to do whatever God wants to help someone else. God has used Malcolm in lots of people's lives. Maybe he's going to use him in Russ's, too."

Nick just shook his head.

"Did you believe anything Malcolm said last night?" she asked cautiously.

"No," Nick said. "I mean, last night it was easy to believe what he was saying because the music and singing kinda got under my skin. But when I got home and thought about it, I could see it was all just a bunch of nonsense."

"Like what?" Addie asked.

"He said if you just ask, God will answer your prayers."

"He will."

Nick paused. "Do you pray for Miss T.?"

Addie nodded, even though she could see what was coming.

"Then why hasn't God answered your prayers and helped her out of this mess?" he asked.

Addie took a deep breath and swallowed. "Nick, when you ask your folks for something, they always give you an answer, don't they?"

He nodded.

"Is it always the answer you want?"

Nick stared ahead, refusing to look at her. She went on.

"God's the same way. He always gives us an answer, but it's not always the one we want. He might want us to wait before He gives us an answer. Or, He might want to use us as part of the answer."

"What?"

"Maybe God's using us to help Miss T. get the money she needs to be able to stay at home." She paused. "Does that make any sense?"

Nick shook his head. "It seems like He's making something that could be real easy into something real hard. I mean, why does Miss T. have to go through all this worrying if God's going to work it out in the end? Why didn't He just do that to begin with?"

Sometimes Addie didn't understand that herself, so she thought carefully before she answered. Finally she told the truth.

"I don't know. Unless it's for the same reason your parents make you go through problems they could solve. To help you learn something."

"God should be better at it than parents."

Nothing more was said until they approached Nick's house. "Will I see you tomorrow?" Addie asked.

"Of course," he said. "I'm sorry, Addie. I don't mean to hurt your feelings. But I can't agree with you about God, so don't try to make me, okay?"

"Okay," she said. "I mean, it's not a requirement for being my friend or anything. But the Lord is the best thing in my life. I just wish you knew Him, too."

"Thanks," Nick said, "but no thanks." He pulled into his driveway and Addie rode on alone.

The next morning she woke early and slipped downstairs to have a quiet time with her mother. She told Mrs. McCormick about the conversation with Nick and they prayed together. Before Addie left, Mrs McCormick laid her hand on the girl's shoulder.

"Don't push Nick, Addie. He trusts you. He showed you that yesterday by telling you as much as he did. When he wants to tell you more, he will. Let him go at his own pace. Okay?"

Addie nodded. "He can't keep me from praying, can he?"

Her mother laughed. "No, honey, he can't. And God will honor your prayers as much as any words you might say."

Nick was waiting for Addie in front of his house. Instead of stopping, she zipped past, but he caught up with her quickly. They raced to the corner turn to Miss T.'s house and shot past it. Addie beat him by a hair.

"That shows you who's fastest," she teased as they doubled back.

"What do you mean?" he protested. "You had a head start!"

"Come on," she said "We haven't seen Miss T. for a couple of days. Let's see if she's baked any chocolate chip cookies lately."

They turned the corner to her house and Addie's throat tightened with fear. Even from a distance, they could see a trail of black smoke drifting out the kitchen window

CHAPTER 11

A Trip
to the Attic

"Please let her be all right, Lord, please let her be all right," Addie mumbled over and over as they raced the half-mile to the old house. Dropping their bikes at the back porch they tore up the steps and peered inside. On the stove, a pan of grease popped angrily. A pile of newspapers on the window sill next to the stove had caught on fire from the burning fat, and they in turn had ignited the curtains.

"Miss T.," Addie shouted through the screen. "Miss T., where are you?"

Footsteps sounded behind them and they turned to see Miss T. hurrying down the path from the greenhouse.

"What's happened, what's happened?" she exclaimed as she ran up the steps and pushed the children aside. "Oh, thank God it hasn't spread." Addie didn't bother to correct her language. "Hurry, Nick, run to the greenhouse and get the fire extinguisher!"

Nick was back in seconds. Miss T. opened the door cautiously and went inside. Spraying the curtains and papers first, she put the fire out quickly. Then she reached over to turn off the stove and used an old towel to push the pan off the burner. "Ouch!" she exclaimed, jerking back from the sizzling grease. She rubbed her arm briskly with the towel and sat down hard.

Addie and Nick came in the house then, staring at the sooty mess on the window and wall.

"How could this have happened?" Miss T. sounded near tears. "I know I checked that burner before I went outside. I—I must have turned the heat up, not down. Dear, dear me."

Just then, a car pulled into the drive. Nick glanced out the window and groaned. Soon Francine's face was peering through the screen.

"Aunt Eunice, I saw smoke . . . oh, Aunt Eunice," she said. Stepping into the kitchen, she stared in disbelief at the charred curtains and newspaper ashes. Then the expression on her face hardened, and she turned to Miss T. with her jaw set.

Miss T. spoke before Francine had a chance. "Children, why don't you come back this afternoon? Francine and I have some things to talk over. Maybe you can help me clean up this mess later."

Addie nodded and the two slipped out the back door.

"What are we going to do?" Nick asked as they pedaled toward home. "This was just the kind of thing Francine was waiting for. I bet she's trying to strong-arm Miss T. out of the house right now!"

"Don't be so dramatic!" Addie said. "You know it takes time to move anywhere. How long did it take your family to get ready? It's not like she'll be gone tomorrow. We still have a little time to work."

"We'd better work fast," Nick said.

When they returned that afternoon, they found Miss T. standing on a chair, scrubbing the window. She motioned them in and stepped down with a grunt. "I decided I couldn't wait for you. The mess and the smell were more than I could stand. Here," she handed Addie the sponge, "why don't you clean the rest of the window. Nick, you've got to move this stove for me. There's grease all down the wall."

Addie finished scrubbing and Nick helped the old woman clean behind the stove. All the time they worked, Miss T. kept up a steady stream of conversation.

"I made cookies last night. I don't suppose either of you would want any. Or a glass of lemonade. Well, we'll just finish here and maybe I'll put you to work scrubbing my basement floor. It hasn't been cleaned for months. This whole house could use a good cleaning. I just don't have the energy to do it anymore." She stopped abruptly and Nick blurted out,

"You're not leaving are you, Miss T.? Can she make you leave?"

Miss T. patted his head roughly and gave him a tired smile. "Francine can't *make* me do anything, Mr. Brady."

"You didn't answer the question," Addie said softly.

"What?" Miss T. asked.

"You didn't answer the question."

"Pretty impertinent, aren't you, miss? Besides, what business is it of yours if I decide to leave?"

Addie stepped down from the chair and dropped her sponge in the bucket with a soft plop. Nick stared at the floor and shuffled his feet.

"I'm sorry. That was uncalled for," Miss T. said. "You children have been the best friends I've had for a long while. I'm just feeling out of sorts today."

Addie and Nick stared at her, silently, waiting.

"Well, what am I *supposed* to do?" she sputtered. "I can't hear a blessed thing anymore, I forget appointments I make, and I almost burned my house down today. Maybe I'd be better off in some old folks home."

"Couldn't you have someone come live with you and help you?" Addie asked.

"How can I do that, child?" she replied. "I barely have enough money to take care of myself, much less pay someone else to do it."

"Don't you have anything you could sell?" Nick asked.

Miss T.'s startled expression made him stammer, "My grandma had some bonds she cashed in so she could go on a trip once."

The suspicion faded from her eyes and she shook her head. "No, no bonds. There, there," she admonished them. "Don't look so worried. This will work out. I'm not sure how, but it will. Well," she said smartly, "let's get back to the job at hand." She turned to study the window. "I need that old pair of curtains I had. Where did I put those? Oh, yes, the attic. Well, I'm too tired to traipse up those stairs today. I'll get them tomorrow."

"Let us get them for you," Nick pleaded. Too desperate to be tactful, he went on, "We've never seen your attic before. We just want to look around. You know how nosy we are."

Miss T. laughed outright at the boy's bluntness and Addie stared at him in amazement. "All right, Mr. Brady," the old woman relented," but don't snoop around too much. There's not much there, and I don't want what little I have messed up. Well, go on," she prodded when they just stood there, "the curtains are green and they're in the trunk by the east window."

Addie took the stairs two at a time with Nick on her heels.

"I can't believe she fell for that!" Addie said as they started up the second flight.

"Me, neither," panted Nick. "Unless," he said as they burst through the attic door and surveyed the empty room in dismay, "unless there's really nothing up here."

CHAPTER 12

The Secret Room

The attic was long and narrow. Light filtered in through the small, broken windows on the north end of the house. The trunk sat next to the only window on the east side, and a variety of boxes and sacks were scattered everywhere else. Addie and Nick sifted through all of them, but found nothing of value hidden there.

Russ was right. The antiques were gone. Addie closed up the last box and sat down on it, trying to fight back the despair she felt. Nick made no such effort.

"I guess this is it, then," he said. "Whatever she was hiding up here is gone. There's nothing we can do."

"I'm not giving up," Addie said stubbornly.

"Face it, Addie," Nick answered. "Whatever Miss T. had that might have been valuable is gone."

"How do we know that? We don't know what she had to begin with!"

Nick grabbed an old white rag from one of the sacks and shook it in Addie's face. "You think Russ is going to pay her big money for tea towels!?"

She grabbed the towel and threw it to the floor. "No," she said as she headed for the stairs, "but I think Russ is a pretty smart cookie. He's convinced Miss T. knows where this stuff is even if it isn't here. *He's* not giving up, and we can't either."

She came to an abrupt halt at the top of the stairs and Nick bumped into her.

"I wish you wouldn't do that," he fumed. "I'm always running into you. What's the matter?"

Addie studied the west side of the house with a perplexed look on her face. She pointed slowly to the window on the east and then back west. "I thought there was a window on this side of the house, too," she said. They stared at the solid wall and a slow smile spread over the young girl's face. "I *know* there's a window here, Nick, I've seen it before!"

Nick cocked an eyebrow and put his hand to her forehead. "No, no fever," he said. "Looks like a wall to me, Addie."

She pushed his hand away. "Don't be smart. Don't you understand? It's *behind* this wall. There must be a secret room!" She paced off the distance between the wall and the stairwell. "See, this is only about six feet and you know the kitchen is wider than that."

"You're right!" Nick exclaimed. "But where's the door? How do you get in?"

"I've seen these in old movies," Addie answered. "The panels are fit together so well you can't see the joints, but there's a spring on one that opens it and it slides behind the others." She began going over the wall with both hands, feeling carefully for any crack or bump that seemed unusual.

"We're not in the movies, Addie," Nick said. "This is real life."

"Here it is!" she whispered. She ran her fingers up and down the crack that followed the grain pattern in the dark paneling. There was a catch at the bottom and the panel popped backwards. She pushed it sideways and it creaked loudly, but neither of them noticed.

Light streamed through the west window that was now revealed. Addie stepped slowly through the opening. Nick followed her and together they surveyed the secret room.

Things were everywhere. A child's sled stood upright against the window. A platform rocker and a small table graced the middle of the room. Three bells sat on the table next to a kerosene lamp. There was a desk in one corner with an old-fashioned inkwell and quill pen. A slip of paper showed out the top of one of the drawers, but they were all locked. An ornate sword hung on one wall and a rack of clothes lined the other. There was a large wicker basket filled with plastic flowers next to a top hat and cane, books, dishes, vases—Addie soon felt overwhelmed trying to sort it all out.

Nick spoke first. "This is priceless? Old, yeah. But priceless?"

Addie was shaking her head. "I don't know, Nick. There's something eery about all this. I feel like it's important for some reason."

"Important to Miss T., maybe."

"No, it's . . . I don't know." She began to work her way around the room, examining different objects, and Nick did the same. Soon they were both covered with dust.

Addie came to the rack of clothes. They were faded and stiff from years of exposure to the dry, dusty air, but some of the dresses were still beautiful. Addie reached in to pull out a flowing red gown and caught her breath. A chill went down her spine and her hands began to shake.

"Nick," she was barely able to whisper, "we *are* in the movies!"

"What?"

Angry voices floated up through the floorboards and both children jumped.

"We've got to get out of here!" Nick pulled Addie toward the door and together they managed to pull the spring panel back into place.

They started down the stairs but Addie turned back and ran into Nick once more.

"What now?" he hissed.

"We forgot the curtains!"

"Oh yeah!"

Curtains in hand, they raced down the two flights of stairs to the kitchen. Miss T. was nowhere in sight, but loud voices were coming from the dining room. Addie and Nick dropped the curtains on the table and hurried through the house to the front room.

Miss T. and Russ Krueger stood face to face. The old woman snatched an envelope, yellowed with age, from Russ's hand and he gave it up without protest. He looked unperturbed as usual, but Miss T.'s fists were clenched and she was so angry she was shaking.

"Let go of the past, lady," he said rudely. "No one cares anymore."

"I care," she said fiercely. "Get out of my house!"

Russ bowed slightly, gave the children a nod and walked out the front door. Miss T. watched him from the window until his car disappeared down the road.

"I'm sorry you had to see that, children," she said. She laid the envelope on her desk, but a breeze caught it and blew it gently to the floor. Nick stooped to pick it up and glanced surreptitiously at the front before laying it back on the desk.

"Mr. Krueger sells antiques," she continued, "and he pesters every old person he finds. He is under the impression if you're over 65, you must own something valuable."

"Why did you even let him in the house?" Nick asked.

"I didn't," Miss T. snapped. "I heard a noise in the front room and found him at my desk. He said he knocked, but when no one answered, he thought he should check on me. Humph. He's never been concerned about my welfare before!"

"Is that important?" Addie nodded toward the envelope.

Miss T. picked it up and crumpled it slowly with one hand. She tossed it in the wastebasket and shook her head. "Not anymore," she said softly. "Children, I'm very tired. Why don't you go home now?"

"Your curtains are on the kitchen table," Nick said. "Do you want us to hang them?"

"Maybe tomorrow," Miss T. answered.

"Let's go, Nick," Addie urged. "Bye, Miss T." She hurried Nick through the house and out the back door. They were barely on their bikes before Addie burst out, "Did you see that red dress in the secret room?"

"Yeah, so? What were you talking about, being in the movies?"

"Nick, I've seen that dress before! Monica wore it in a movie called 'The Lady Wore Red.'"

"Monica who?"

"I don't know 'Monica who'! That was just her name in the movie. What difference does that make? Anyway," Addie continued, "I think those are all old movie props. That top hat and cane? Jeffrey wore those to the White House in 'Spys for Sale.' And don't ask me Jeffrey who," she said quickly. "Just Jeffrey. And I think that's the sword Sir Arnold carried in 'Knights of Splendor.' I never saw the movie, but it's one of my dad's favorites. He showed me a picture of Sir Arnold with that sword in one of his movie books." She ran out of breath and Nick jumped into the conversation while he had the chance.

"Why would Miss T. have all this stuff? I mean, if it's authentic, she must know how valuable it is. Why wouldn't she want to sell it? She could be rich!"

"I don't think the question is, 'Why won't she sell it?' I think the question is, 'How did she get it?'" Addie looked at Nick and he nodded.

"'You don't wanna know, kid,'" he said.

"Right." Addie began to feel a knot of fear take hold in her stomach again, and she asked softly, "Nick, are we in over our heads?"

CHAPTER 13

The Lady Wore Red

"Now who's being dramatic?" Nick scoffed. "You still haven't convinced me those are old movie props."

"All right, smartie," she said. "Let's go. My dad's got tons of books on this stuff. I'll show you the picture of Sir Arnold with that sword."

"Addie, just because it looks like the sword in the picture, doesn't mean it *is* the sword in the picture."

"What about the dress, Nick? And all those other things? I recognize a lot of them, now. It's just too much of a coincidence."

"Maybe she's an old movie buff like your dad. Maybe she bought replicas of those things when she was growing up. I mean, I've got a light saber from the movie 'Star Wars,' but so do about five million other kids."

"The old movies weren't commercialized like ones today are. I doubt if the producers even marketed replicas to sell to the public. Besides, why would Miss T. hide them in a secret room in the attic?"

Nick sighed. "You can sure be stubborn."

"Only when I'm right," Addie muttered.

"Well, excuuuuuuuse me," he said.

They got to Addie's house and found Mrs. McCormick in the kitchen.

"Mom, do you think Dad would care if we looked at some of his movie books?"

"I'm sure he wouldn't, dear. Just put them back when you're done."

Addie led Nick upstairs to the study, and pulled two large volumes from the bookcase above Mr. McCormick's desk. One was titled *Hollywood's Finest* and the other was *Those Were The Days*. She spent several minutes searching for the picture of Sir Arnold, and Nick drummed his fingers on the desk impatiently.

"Here it is!" She pointed to the picture in question and Nick studied it closely. There was really no doubt, though. The sword Sir Arnold carried was the sword on Miss T.'s attic wall.

"Let me see if I can find a picture of that dress," Addie continued. "I just saw the movie a few weeks ago. It should be in here..." She looked in the index under "The Lady Wore Red" and flipped quickly to the reference. The picture showed a stunning actress with bright blue eyes and black hair staring imperiously at the camera. The red dress she wore looked exactly like the dress in Miss T.'s attic.

"What about that hat and cane?" Nick asked, still skeptical.

Addie found "Spys for Sale" in short order and pointed silently to a dapper-looking man holding the top hat and cane.

"Okay." Nick finally relented. "Maybe you're right. But what can we do about it? We can't just waltz in her front door and say 'Miss T., why don't you sell that collection of movie props you've got hidden in your attic?' She might not like that. Especially if she . . ." he hesitated ". . . if she stole them."

"We don't know that she stole them, Nick. I can't believe Miss T. would steal anything. It goes against her character. No, I think there's something else that we're missing."

She turned back to the picture of "Spys for Sale." Holding her finger in the page, she found the reference to "The Lady Wore Red." She was silent for several minutes as she flipped back and forth between the two, reading the information given for both.

"That's interesting," she murmured.

"What?" Nick asked.

"The leading actors were the same in both movies," she replied. "Winston Rinehart and Tierny Bryce. They were a team in those days. I remember the names, Rinehart and Bryce. Kind of like Tracy and Hepburn, only not so famous."

"Like who?" Nick asked.

"Spencer Tracy and Katherine Hepburn," Addie said. Nick's expression was blank and Addie laughed. "I guess you have to have a father who watches old movies to know any of these people. They were all real famous 40 years ago."

"I'll take your word for it," Nick said.

"Wait a minute." Addie found the picture of Sir Arnold and the sword once more. She scanned the page quickly and nodded. "Yep. Rinehart and Bryce again. That's got to be important, but I don't know why!"

She sat back and the book flopped open to the picture of "The Lady Wore Red."

Nick glanced at it casually and said, "She reminds me of Francine."

Addie jerked upright in her chair and grabbed the book. "Nick, we must be blind!"

"Why?"

"Who does Francine look like?"

"Miss—" Nick's mouth dropped open and he stared at the picture in amazement. "Miss T."

They sat in stunned silence, hardly daring to believe their suspicions. But the bright blue eyes that snapped back at them from the picture could not be mistaken.

"Addie, there's more!" Nick spoke urgently, and his face had drained of all its color. "I knew that name sounded familiar. Remember the envelope Miss T. dropped this afternoon?"

Addie nodded.

"The return address said W. Rinehart!"

CHAPTER 14

Miss T.
... or not Miss T.?

"This is incredible." Addie finally spoke. "I don't believe this is happening."

"You better believe it," Nick said. "I bet Russ Krueger believes it."

"Do you think he suspects Miss T. is..." Addie found it difficult to say the words.

"Tierny Bryce?" Nick shrugged. "We know he suspects she's hiding those props, that's for sure. But he hasn't found them, so he can't do anything about it, no matter what he knows."

"The question is, what can we do about it? How do we go to Miss T. and tell her we've discovered she's an old movie star?" Addie picked up the movie book once more and gazed at the lady in red. "Wasn't she beautiful, Nick?"

Nick nodded. "You have to admit, she's still kind of pretty, for an old lady."

"But she was gorgeous then," Addie said softly.

"She was gorgeous, wasn't she?" a voice behind them said and both children jumped.

Addie's father stood peering over their shoulders. "Why the sudden interest in Tierny Bryce, kiddo? Did you happen to see one of her old pictures on T.V.?"

Addie nodded. "I watched 'The Lady Wore Red' when we first moved here."

"I've taped several of her movies off the public broadcasting television channel, if you're interested in seeing any others," he commented. " 'Spys for Sale' is a pretty good one. She and that Rinehart guy made quite a few pictures," he continued. "They could have been big names in the industry. Too bad." He turned to leave the room.

"Wait a minute!" Addie jumped out of her chair and followed him. "What do you mean, could have been? Too bad what?"

"Tierny Bryce died shortly after 'The Lady Wore Red' was released. Rineharts' career was never the same."

Addie's stomach seemed to dive down to her toes, and she couldn't speak. Nick managed to ask, "How did she die?"

Addie's father pondered the question momentarily and shook his head. "I don't know. I do seem to remember there was some speculation as to whether it was an accident or a murder." He nodded toward *Hollywood's Finest*. "Keep looking. That book should tell you."

He shut the office door as he left, and Addie sank to the sofa. Nick picked up the book and brought it to the couch. Together they found BRYCE, TIERNY, in the index.

It was a long article and Addie scanned it quickly.

Hollywood still mourns the death of Tierny Bryce, one of the finest actresses ever to grace the big screen. When Miss Bryce's body slipped into the depths of Spring Lake that cold October night, the career of Hollywood's most promising duo, Rinehart and Bryce, slipped into obscurity as well . . .

The article was more than three pages long, detailing the career of Tierny Bryce, but it gave no more information concerning her death.

"She drowned," Addie said. "But why did they suspect she had been murdered? If we could get to the library, I bet we could find some newspaper articles from the time that would tell us more." Addie sighed. She was deeply disappointed to find out Tierny Bryce was dead. She studied the lady in red once more. "She sure *looks* like Miss T."

Nick slapped his forehead. "Are we dense, or what? Tierny Bryce could be Miss T.'s sister!"

"Of course!" Addie said. "They look so much alike. And that would explain why Miss T. doesn't want to sell. I'm sure it must be painful to know your sister might have been murdered. She wouldn't want to go through all that again. If she sells those things, the media would be sure to find out and they'd never give her any peace."

"What are you saying?" Nick asked. "There's no solution? If she sells, she loses her privacy. If she doesn't, she loses her home. Which is worse?"

Addie had no answer. The phone rang softly in the living room and they could hear Mr. McCormick answer.

Then the door to the office opened and her father stepped in. "There's quite a storm brewing, kids," he said. "It's already hit the station and done some damage. Your mom and I are going in to see what has to be done to clean it up. You want to go along?"

"Do you mind if we stay here, Dad? We'll be all right."

"I know you will, sweetheart. If it gets bad outside, just unplug everything and head for the basement, okay?" Addie nodded. "Good. We'll be back as soon as we can."

Addie watched from the study window as her parents drove away. The sky had turned a menacing gray, and she could see flashes of lightning in the distance. The wind picked up, and the room turned noticeably darker. Addie reached out to flick on the overhead light.

"There's still a missing piece to the puzzle," she said. "And I think it's in Miss T.'s attic. There must be something we overlooked, something that would make everything else fall into place." She sighed. "But I'm so hungry I can't keep my mind on it. You want a pizza?"

"I'd love it!" Nick said. "I'm starved. Let me call my mom and tell her I'm eating here."

It took them less than half an hour to cook and devour a 12-inch pepperoni pizza. When they were finished, Nick helped Addie clean up the few dishes and then they sat out on the front porch and watched the storm front blow in from the west. It soon became too windy to stay outside and they retreated to the living room. Nick kept a watchful eye on the window.

"I hate these summer storms," he said. "Tornadoes scare me."

"Me, too," Addie agreed. "We never had many in Wisconsin, but there has already been one here this summer."

"You think Miss T. will be okay?" he asked.

"She's lived here 45 years, remember? She's seen storms like this before."

"Forty-five years?" Nick repeated.

Addie nodded. The same thought had occurred to her and she did some quick mental arithmetic. "She moved here the same year Tierny Bryce died."

"Addie, this is getting too weird for me."

"I know." She paused. "Maybe it's time to pray." She said the words softly, almost to herself. Nick heard her and sniffed.

"What good would that do?"

"What good have *we* done?" she retorted. Nick didn't answer, so Addie went on. "My mom said if we just kept praying for Miss T., the Lord would show us what we could do to help her."

Nick remained silent and Addie decided to take that as his agreement to pray. She closed her eyes, folded her hands and plunged in.

"Lord, we don't know where to go from here. There are so many things we don't understand. But you understand it all. And I trust you to take care of Miss T. and work this all out for her good. And please, Lord, show us what we can do to help her. We really like Miss T. . . . a lot." She finished so softly Nick didn't hear her 'amen,' and his eyes remained closed.

At least he prayed, Addie thought.

The phone jangled shrilly and Nick's eyes popped open. He laughed self-consciously. "Maybe that's God."

Addie smacked his arm. "Don't be sacrilegious. Hello?"

"Addie? Addie, is your father home?" It was Miss T. and her voice sounded strained.

"What's the matter, Miss T.?" Addie asked. Lightning flashed and there was a sharp crackle in the phone.

"Addie, are you still there?" The line buzzed and snapped and Addie could barely hear the old woman's voice.

"Addie, please get your father! I need your help. Please!"

"He's not here—" Addie shouted into the receiver, but there was a final loud *Crack!* and the line was dead.

CHAPTER 15

The Storm

Addie was frantic. "What are we going to do, Nick? Something's wrong!"

"Let's go." He was out of the room before Addie could stop him.

"Wait a second. Look at it outside. My parents will have kittens if we go out in this!"

"We can beat the rain, Addie. Leave them a note and say we'll stay there until the storm is over. Better yet, tell them to come to Miss T.'s. We don't know what's happened. We might need help."

Addie scribbled a quick *Miss T. needs help—please come!* on the chalkboard by the fridge, and the two children were out the door. The wind was to their backs and they made the distance to Nick's corner in record time. Even so, Nick stood up to pedal faster as they rode by his house.

"Let's hope my folks don't see us!" he shouted.

They pulled into Miss T.'s driveway just as the rain hit. By the time they reached the back, they were both drenched, but neither of them gave it a thought. Russ Krueger's blue Ford was parked at the end of the drive. For the first time since they had known her, Nick and Addie burst through Miss T.'s back door without knocking.

"Miss T.!" Addie shouted as they raced through the house. They were stopped short by the sight of Miss T. and Russ Krueger working side by side in the dining room. Russ was half-in, half-out of the large north window, working frantically to saw off the branch that protruded through the broken glass. Miss T. was gingerly pulling out the jagged shards left in the frame. When she saw the children, she pointed to the flashlight on the desk.

"Take that and go to the attic. There's a roll of plastic at the top of the stairs. You'll both have to go. It's very heavy. Hurry!"

Addie grabbed the flashlight, and she and Nick raced to the attic. The roll was big, and they were both winded by the time they got back to the dining room. Russ had the plastic stapled over the window in short order, but the wind snapped it angrily. Miss T. found several old boards to nail over it and hold it in place. When he was finished, Russ sat down in the arm chair and took out a handkerchief to mop his wet face and arms.

Miss T. sat down on the sofa. "Thank you all for your help," she said. "I phoned the sheriff, but he was on a call. I tried Francine and her husband, but I couldn't get through. When I talked to you, Addie, and the line went dead, I was frantic. Your arrival was most timely, Mr. Krueger."

"What were you doing here?" Nick blurted out.

"Nicholas!" Miss T.'s voice was sharp with reproof. "Mr. Krueger has very kindly helped me and he deserves thanks, not questions." She paused. "At least, not rude ones."

Russ smiled slightly. "Do you know the Kleiss family, Miss Tisdale?"

The Kleisses farmed the land adjacent to Miss T.'s house, and she and Addie both nodded.

"Mrs. Kleiss wants to sell several antique pieces she inherited from her grandmother, and I was working out details with her this afternoon. I left when the storm started, and drove by your house just as that old tree went down. I knew you would need help, so I stopped."

For the first time since they met Russ, Addie believed him. "That was nice."

"It was very nice," Miss T. agreed. "Thank you for your trouble." There was an awkward silence and then she said, "Can I offer you something to drink?"

Russ shook his head. "No, I should be leaving. They're expecting me back at the store. I'll see myself out."

Miss T. nodded, and they listened as he walked through the house. The back door slammed in the wind. Lightning flashed once more and thunder vibrated the air.

"What a mess," Miss T. sighed. "I was doing work at my desk when the wind picked up. I thought I might need my flashlight so I went to the kitchen to get it. I came back to this room and was barely through the door when that tree went down."

She looked at the broken glass that covered the top of her desk. "I'm lucky I wasn't hurt."

"Lucky, nothing!" Addie couldn't restrain herself. "I think God protected you. Nick and I were praying."

Miss T. patted Addie's cheek. "You think I need your prayers, miss?"

Addie didn't answer, and Miss T. smiled wearily. "You're probably right." She began picking glass up off the floor and Addie knelt to help. "No, no, child, I don't want you to cut yourself."

"We could take the plastic back to the attic for you," Nick offered.

"That would be fine," Miss T. said rather absentmindedly. "I'll get a broom and a sack."

Addie and Nick picked up the roll of plastic. They made slow progress to the attic. Addie still held the flashlight and the beam of light bobbed up and down as they labored up two flights of stairs with their awkward bundle.

Once at the top, they dropped it with a thud. Nick took Addie's arm and pulled her toward the secret room.

"Come on," he whispered. "This might be the only chance we'll have to get back in there." When Addie hesitated, Nick took the flashlight from her hand and began fumbling along the wall to find the spring panel.

"It's right here," Addie said, and the panel popped back under her touch. They stepped through the door and Nick swung the beam of light slowly over the room. Objects that had seemed odd enough in the daylight were downright spooky as lightning flashed and illuminated them momentarily. Addie shivered.

"Wait!" She grabbed the flashlight and directed its beam back to the desk in the corner. She looked more closely at the slip of paper that poked out the top of the drawer. It was a newspaper clipping. Addie gently pulled on one corner. It wouldn't budge. She tried jiggling the drawer, but to no avail. On impulse, she stuck two fingers in the empty inkwell, and touched something cold. Pulling out a small key, she inserted it in the lock. The drawer slid open silently.

Inside, old newspaper clippings filled every inch of space. Addie picked up the top one and read, *TIERNY BRYCE, HOLLYWOOD STARLET, DEAD AT 30.* "This is it, Nick!"

Nick grabbed several more clippings from the drawer. "We don't have time to read them here. Let's go." At the expression on Addie's face, he said, "We'll bring them back, Miss Law-and-Order." He folded the papers hastily and stuffed them in his jeans pocket.

They pulled the door shut and left the attic. Addie flicked off the flashlight, and the light from the second floor landing shone softly at the bottom of the stairs.

Just then, a large shadow fell across the landing. Russ Krueger stepped around the corner.

"I thought I'd find you here," he said softly.

CHAPTER 16

Tierny Bryce

"I thought you left," Addie stammered.

Russ put a finger to his lips and motioned them down the stairs.

"Look, I know what you think about me. Believe it or not, I want to help the old lady, too. But I can't—and you can't—if we don't know where she's keeping ..." He hesitated to say anything more.

"Those things belong to Miss T., and you're not getting your grubby hands on them!" Nick burst out.

Russ jerked back as if he'd been hit. "You found them!" It was a statement, not a question, and there was unveiled excitement in his voice. Addie could have punched Nick.

"I ... I ... Why don't you just leave Miss T. alone?" Nick sputtered.

"Look, kid, why can't I get this through your head? I'm not here to rob the old gal, I just want a chance to make some money myself. If I can get her a good deal, why should you care if I make a few bucks on the side?"

"You mean you don't want to blackmail her?" Addie asked.

Russ looked puzzled. "Why would I blackmail her?"

"I thought you knew how she got those... things," Nick said.

Russ regarded the two children soberly. "That's better left unsaid."

"You can't sell everything and expect it to be left unsaid," Addie exclaimed.

"I've got the right connections, kid, trust me. But I have to know where the stuff is hidden!" His voice rose in frustration.

The two children remained silent, and Russ shook his head. Taking a card from his front pocket, he handed it to Addie. "If you decide you want to help your precious Miss T., give me a call." He turned and padded softly down the steps.

Addie and Nick followed him. This time, Addie stood at the back door and watched his car pull away. The rain dimmed his headlights and they disappeared quickly down the road. Miss T. came into the kitchen. She put the sack of broken glass inside another sack and closed it up tightly.

"I'll have to have Willard and Francine get the big pieces tomorrow," she said. She shook her head at the sight of the two wet, bedraggled children before her. Addie was suddenly conscious of the newspaper clipping she still held in one hand and Russ Krueger's business card in the other. She put her hands behind her back as inconspicuously as possible and smiled.

"Did you get it all cleaned up?" she asked.

"No," Miss T. answered. She opened the large cupboard by the door and took out an armful of rags. "I need to mop up the water."

"We'll help," Nick offered, but Miss T. shook her head.

"No, there's still too much glass around," she answered. "Addie, why don't you put water on to boil while I finish up? I could use a nice strong cup of tea." She tossed two large rags on the table. "And dry yourselves off before you sit down."

"Sure," Addie said. She tucked the papers in the back pocket of her shorts and toweled off quickly. She put the tea kettle on the stove, then pulled out a chair and sat down at the table.

"I've got to look at this article, Nick," Addie said. "You watch the door."

Nick backed up and stood in the doorway. He listened as Addie read the article in a whisper.

TIERNY BRYCE,
HOLLYWOOD STARLET, DEAD AT 30

The bright red roadster that was Tierny Bryce's trademark was found submerged in Spring Lake early Friday morning, October 15. Friends had reported her missing Thursday when she did not arrive for work on the set of her latest picture. Authorities went to her home to investigate late Thursday night and discovered tire tracks down the steep incline that leads from Miss Bryce's estate to a 10-foot drop-off over the lake's edge. The automobile was recovered at approximately 4 A.M. Friday morning.

Skid marks at the top of the incline have lead to early reports that Miss Bryce returned to her estate traveling at high speeds and lost control of her car when she attempted to brake.

Tierny Bryce was last seen Wednesday afternoon at the famed "Club Royale." Several witnesses claim the renowned actress was involved in an argument with an unknown man. This has led to much speculation concerning foul play in the actress's death. However, authorities have no leads as to the identity of Miss Bryce's escort at Club Royale and have not filed any charges, pending further investigation.

Meanwhile, divers continue to search for the body of the late actress.

"Nick," Addie said urgently, "let me see some of the clippings you took. Hurry!"

Nick pulled the crumpled papers from his front pocket and laid them on the table. Addie scanned through them all and picked up one that read *MEMORIAL SERVICE FOR TIERNY BRYCE.*

"All of Hollywood met today..." she mumbled, "...hundreds of Hollywood's finest...homage to a great actress...mystery still surrounds...Here it is!" Addie read silently for several moments and Nick poked her.

"Come on, Addie, what's it say?"

"'More accurate details of the actress's death will never be known. Divers discontinued their search for the body Sunday afternoon.'"

"You mean they never found her body?" Nick asked.

"Of course not," Addie said softly.

"Why not?"

"Because, Mr. Brady," said Miss T. from the doorway, "I'm a very good swimmer."

CHAPTER 17

Addie's Explanation

Miss T. pulled out the chair next to Addie and sat down. "Have a seat, Mr. Brady," she said. Nick sat down across from Addie and stared at his hands. Addie busied herself collecting the clippings that lay scattered across the table.

Miss T. waited until Addie finished stacking and folding the papers into a neat pile. Then she commanded, "Look at me, miss."

Addie forced herself to meet the woman's gaze. "I'm sorry, Miss T. We were only trying to help."

Miss T. nodded. "I know, child." She sighed. "I've been expecting this day for more than 45 years." She shook her head. "But never in my wildest imagination did I expect to be found out by two nosy children!"

Addie slid down slightly in her chair and Nick turned crimson.

"Have you told anyone what you know?" Miss T. asked.

"Oh, no!" they protested, and Miss T. held up her hand.

"I believe you. However, if you've discovered the truth, Mr. Krueger will not be far behind. Francine has kept my secret for many years, but I can't expect that any longer." She paused. "I do feel you owe me an explanation. Would you like to begin or should we wait for your father?"

Addie glanced out the window after Miss T. and groaned. Her father's car pulled down the drive and stopped by the back door. Nick folded both arms on the table and buried his head.

Miss T. opened the door and Mr. McCormick's anxious face peered in through the screen. "Miss Tisdale? Hi, I'm John McCormick. Is my daughter—" He stopped when he saw Addie at the table. "There you are! We were a little worried when we saw your note."

Miss T. opened the screen and Mr. McCormick shook out his umbrella before stepping inside. The rain had all but stopped. The moon was slipping out from behind a cloud.

"Is everything all right?" he asked. "The note said you needed some help."

"Yes," Miss T. answered. "That old oak on the north side of the house finally came down in the wind. One of its branches went through my dining room window. The children were kind enough to help me clean up the mess. However," she continued, "we are discussing something far more important right now. Something I want you to hear, Mr. McCormick. If your daughter is any reflection of you, I believe you are a man to be trusted."

Mr. McCormick looked puzzled, but he sat down without any questions.

"Okay, shoot."

Miss T. looked at Addie. The young girl took a deep breath and began.

"The first day Nick and I met you, we saw a man in your attic window. He left through the woods and we tried to tell you about him, but you wouldn't listen."

Nick picked up the story. "We followed him and saw his car, a dark blue Ford. About a week later we were outside when we heard you arguing with someone in the kitchen. There was a blue car in your drive, but it wasn't the mystery man, only Francine. That's when we found out about you going to a retirement home . . ."

" . . . And about the antiques in your attic," Addie interjected.

"Then we went to a rally and met Russ Krueger. He's the man who was in the attic," Nick said for Mr. McCormick's benefit. "When we found out he was an antique dealer, we thought you must have some antiques Russ wanted."

"The next day we found him trying to break into your house, so we knew it was something serious," Addie said. "But we still didn't know what you had. It was about that time you had the fire . . ."

"And we knew Francine was going to force you to leave your house if we didn't do something fast," Nick interrupted. "We thought if we could find the antiques and talk you into selling them, you could hire someone to stay here with you, instead of going into a home. So we got into your attic—"

"What!?" Addie's father exclaimed.

"We had permission, Dad," Addie interrupted hastily. "We looked around, but couldn't find anything that looked like antiques. Then I noticed that the west wall of the attic was solid, but I was sure I'd seen a window from the outside. I thought the wall must be fake, so we started looking for a hidden door."

"Addie found it right away, too," Nick said proudly.

"That's when we found the secret room and all the—the—" Addie stammered to a halt. She gave Miss T. a questioning look, and the old woman nodded.

"The what, Addie?" her father prodded.

"Remember the picture we looked at this afternoon, Dad? Tierny Bryce in 'The Lady Wore Red'?"

Mr. McCormick nodded.

"We found that dress—and lots of other stuff."

Addie's father looked quickly to the old woman and Miss T. nodded again. "At first I didn't recognize all the things that were there," Addie continued. "But when I saw the red dress, other things started to look familiar. I had to prove to Nick they were authentic. That's why we had your old movie books out."

Nick picked up the story. "When I took a closer look at the picture of Tierny Bryce, I said, 'She looks like Francine,' who looks like Miss T., and then it hit us. Miss T. was Tierny Bryce!"

Mr. McCormick sat upright in his chair and stared at Miss T.

"Then you came in and told us Tierny Bryce was dead," Addie said.

Her father relaxed slightly and placed one hand on his forehead. No one spoke for several seconds and he looked up.

"Go on," he said. "I'm listening. I can't believe what I'm hearing, but I'm listening."

"So we suspected Tierny Bryce was Miss T.'s sister," Nick said.

"That would have explained a lot," Addie said, "but I couldn't get rid of the feeling that we were missing something. Then the storm started and Miss T. called for help, so we came over. She needed plastic from the attic to cover the broken window. When we took it back upstairs we went to the secret room again and found these newsclippings." Addie pointed to the piles on the table.

"They're all about Tierny Bryce's death," Nick said.

"And you were right, Dad. They were never able to decide if her death was an accident or a murder, because—" Addie took a deep breath—"because they never found her body."

Mr. McCormick could only shake his head as Miss. T. extended her hand. He shook it.

"How do you do, Mr. McCormick?" she asked.

"How do you do, Miss Bryce?" he answered faintly.

CHAPTER 18

The
Whole Story

Mr. McCormick sat in silence for several long minutes and Addie squirmed under his somber gaze. Finally he spoke.

"Would you be willing to answer a question, Miss—?"

"Call me Eunice. That has always been my legal name, Eunice Tisdale. Tierny Bryce was only a stage name and I never adopted it legally. As to your question, I will do my best. What is it?"

Mr. McCormick seemed to struggle for the right words. Finally he shrugged. "Why?"

"Why did I leave?"

He nodded.

"My life was not my own in those days, Mr. McCormick. At the time, I was under contract to the studio and even though I was considered a major star, I had no choice in the roles they gave me. As I can be a rather strong-willed person..."

Both children grinned at the understatement, and Miss T. gave Addie's dark hair a slight tug before continuing.

". . . I was constantly at odds with my producers. That was a difficult situation at best, but when they began arranging my social life as well, I grew increasingly unhappy."

"What did they do?" Addie asked.

"They started rumors of romance between myself and Winston Rinehart, my co-star. Winston and I were the best of friends, but never anything more. Winston was, in fact, head-over-heels in love with a woman named Caroline, one of the extras from 'Spys for Sale.' When the studio insisted we attend several premiers and parties as a 'couple,' it put quite a strain on both of us.

"I went to the studio and asked to be released from my contract. Of course they refused, and even threatened me with legal action. When I indicated I might be willing to fight them in court and reveal the truth about Winston and I, they sent a man to . . . uhm, shall we say, persuade me to rethink my position."

"Was that the man you were arguing with at the Club Royale?" Nick asked.

Miss T. nodded. "I was very upset after our conversation and did exactly what the investigators suspected. I drove home at a frightful speed and lost control of my car at the top of that hill. I skidded down the embankment and into the lake. Fortunately, I was able to free myself before the car sank. When I calmed down, and dried off, it occurred to me I had a perfect way out of the whole ugly mess.

"I called the one person I knew I could trust in all of Hollywood. He helped me get out of town and to my sister's house unnoticed." She gestured to the room around them. "Martha had been recently widowed. She was struggling to raise Francine and conveniently, 'inherited' my estate. We lived here in peace for more than 40 years. Martha passed away about five years ago, and I have been alone ever since. That is, until I met Mr. Krueger . . . and you." She cocked one eyebrow at the children.

"How did Russ find out about your things?" Nick asked.

"Jack Krueger, Russ's uncle, is the dear friend who helped me stage my 'death.' Jack was the director of all of my movies and often sold me mementos from the films when they were completed. At the time, no one saw any value in them, but I was sentimental and they meant a lot to me. Years later, at a family reunion, Jack let it slip that 'Tierny Bryce' collected props from her movies. Of course, being an antique dealer, Russ was fascinated. He was thrilled to discover my sister lived so near his business, and it was easy for him to trace our family to this house. He's been nosing around for more than a year now, but never made it into the house until the day you saw him in the attic."

"Does Russ know there was never a death?" Addie asked.

Miss T. shook her head. "Not yet. He assumes I am the sister. Fortunately, he was not as curious as you and never discovered the hidden room. But he seems to come closer to the truth every day, and I'm not sure what he would do with that knowledge if he had it."

No one spoke. Miss T. sighed, "As you can see, Mr. McCormick, I am now in quite difficult circumstances. The children are right, of course. Selling my mementos is the most sensible thing to do. I do not want to leave my home." She paused and then said, "But the idea of dealing with all that publicity after 45 years is almost more than I can bear."

"We're sorry, Miss T.," Addie apologized once more. "I guess we got carried away with our mystery. We only wanted to help you. We didn't think there might be . . . consequences." She avoided her father's stern gaze.

"Could you get in trouble with the law if anyone finds out you're Tierny Bryce?" Nick asked.

Miss T. smiled. "I don't think so, child. As I said, I never changed my name legally. The *name* Tierny Bryce is dead, but Eunice Tisdale has been alive and well . . . and paying taxes, I might add . . . for 75 years."

"Perhaps your niece could sell the props for you," Mr. McCormick suggested.

Miss T. shook her head. "How would she explain their sudden appearance after so many years? The press would be on her like a duck on a junebug. They wouldn't let up until they found out the truth. Even if she managed to keep my secret, Russ would not be so accommodating, I'm afraid. He would lead them straight to this house."

"I've spoken with Russ on numerous occasions," Mr. McCormick said, "and I think he could be persuaded to help you. If it was profitable for him, that is. Would you mind if I make a few phone calls, Miss T.?"

She pursed her lips and studied the younger man for several moments. Finally she nodded. "Please do. I appreciate your help, Mr. McCormick."

"It's the least I can do, since my daughter is partially responsible for your predicament." He glanced at Addie once more and the young girl squirmed in her chair.

"I can't promise anything," Mr. McCormick continued, "but there just might be a way Eunice Tisdale can stay in her home and Tierny Bryce can stay in her grave."

CHAPTER 19

The Reunion

The ride home was extremely quiet. When Mr. McCormick pulled into Nick's drive, Addie turned to face him. "We're in major trouble, right?"

Mr. McCormick smiled slightly at the expression on his daughter's face. "Well, honey, as I think you learned tonight, there are always consequences to your actions. So if you're asking me if I'm going to enforce some consequences, yes I am."

Addie flopped back in her seat and Nick sighed.

"I know how easy it must have been to get caught up in the excitement of all this, but part of growing up is looking ahead and thinking about how your behavior will affect the people around you."

"We had no idea she was a movie star, Dad! We just thought she had some valuable antiques. How could we have known it would lead to this?"

"You couldn't, honey. But you *did* know Miss T. didn't want all that 'help' you gave her."

Nick nodded slowly. "I guess we should have backed off. But if we hadn't..."

Mr. McCormick held up his hand. "Don't waste time now trying to second-guess all the decisions you made. What's done is done, and we have to work from where we're at. But remember what you've learned from this the next time you try to help someone who might not want—or need—your help."

"Okay." Addie hesitated. "Are you going to keep her secret, Dad?"

Mr. McCormick looked surprised. "Well, I'm going to tell your mother, of course, but other than that, yes I am. What would make you think otherwise?"

"Is that the right thing to do?" Nick asked.

This time Mr. McCormick sighed. "Boy, that's a tough one." He took a deep breath. "I don't agree with the decisions Miss T. made that got her where she is today. I think by solving one problem with her alleged 'death,' she created several others. But she has to choose how to deal with her problems. I can't make those choices for her. And that's what I'd be doing if I were to tell anyone her story."

"Isn't it wrong to help her keep up the deception?"

"That's not what we're doing, Addie. Certain people will have to know the truth. And that means there's a risk others might find out. Miss T. understands that. No, I said there's a chance we could keep Tierny Bryce at rest."

"What's the difference?" Addie was confused.

"Honey, just because you have certain information doesn't mean you have to give that information to the world." He paused. "Do you remember when Hal came to church and asked us for prayer for his alcoholism?"

Addie nodded.

"Did you go out the next day and tell everyone about his problem?"

"Of course not!" Addie said.

"Why not?"

"Well," Addie said, "that's private. I mean, he trusted us."

"Exactly. Now, there might come a time when Hal tells other people himself. But that's his responsibility, not ours. It's our responsibility to pray for him. Can you see the similarities in Miss T.'s situation?"

Addie nodded. "I guess we need to be . . . discreet?"

Mr. McCormick smiled. "That's a good word. And if we use discretion here, I think we can help Miss T. a great deal."

"How?" Nick asked.

He laughed. "I haven't figured out the details myself, Nick. You're going to have to wait and see."

The next day was Saturday, and Mr. McCormick spent the entire morning in his study on the phone. He drove Addie and Nick to Miss T.'s around noon to pick up their bikes. Although they plied him with questions all the way there, he would only say that everything was falling into place. When they arrived at Miss T.'s he made the children leave almost immediately. He stayed behind to talk to Miss T. and didn't arrive home until after 1 o'clock.

"If I know my father, this is probably part of my punishment," Addie said to Nick as they sat on her front porch and waited.

"What is?" Nick asked.

"He's keeping me in the dark about what's going on," Addie said. "He knows it drives me nuts."

The screen door squeaked open, and Mrs. McCormick stepped outside to join the children. Addie and her father had spent more than an hour the night before repeating the whole story for her mother. Mrs. McCormick laughed now at the gloom in her daughter's voice.

"You've been in the thick of things once too often, dear," she said. "I think your father wants you to learn your lesson."

Addie rolled her eyes at Nick. "What did I tell you?" she said.

Just then, Mr. McCormick pulled into the driveway. The children followed him into the house and waited expectantly as he poured himself a glass of iced tea.

"Well!?" Addie finally burst out. "What's going on?"

Mr. McCormick grinned. "We're all invited to supper at Miss T.'s Monday night." He paused. "That's all you need to know. Now act like normal kids for the next two days, will you? Go . . . climb a tree or something." He refused to say anything more.

Monday finally arrived. At Mrs. McCormick's insistence, Addie and Nick dressed in their best clothes. They all arrived at Miss T.'s house 15 minutes early.

Miss T. was ready for them. The entire house had been dusted and cleaned. China and silverware Addie had never seen before graced the dining room table. There were candles lit and wonderful smells came from the kitchen.

But it was Miss T. herself that stopped Addie short. The thick grey hair that was always in a tight bun at the back of her neck had been loosened slightly and fastened with a plain gold clasp. She wore a light blue dress that matched her eyes, and a single strand of pearls with tiny pearl earrings. She carried herself with the same dignity the children had always seen, but there was a softness about her tonight that made them stare at her in wonder.

"Oh, stop," she said in the voice they knew so well. Addie giggled. Same old Miss T.

And yet she wasn't quite the same. Although she tried to make conversation, Addie could tell her thoughts were somewhere else. She kept glancing out the window and rearranging the flowers on the table. She made several trips to the kitchen to check the roast and Addie went with her to help carry out the drinks. Miss T. poured water for eight people, and Addie was puzzled.

"Who else is coming?" she asked. As if in answer to her question, a long black limousine with shaded windows pulled into the drive and stopped by the front door.

"What?" Miss T. asked, busy with the gravy.

"Never mind," Addie said. She strained to see out the kitchen window.

Russ Krueger was the first to step out of the car. Another older man stepped out the passenger's side, and Addie could see the family resemblance.

"That must be Jack Krueger," she said to herself. Then a third person stepped out of the back seat and Addie's heart began to pound.

Winston Rinehart was a tall man with beautiful silver-grey hair. His eyes looked almost black beneath his bushy eyebrows and his posture was ramrod straight. Although 45 years had passed, Addie could still see Sir Arnold in the older man's expression and it took her breath away.

She heard a knock at the front door, and then her father's voice welcoming the visitors. Footsteps sounded down the hall and Addie braced herself.

"Hand me that bowl on the table, will you, dear?" Miss T. asked.

But Winston Rinehart was in the doorway and Addie couldn't speak.

Miss T. looked over her shoulder and stopped stirring gravy at the sight of Addie's face. "What is it, child?"

"It's me, Tee."

For the first time since Addie had known her, Miss T.'s hearing worked like a charm. She whirled around to see Winston Rinehart standing in her kitchen door.

"Winston!" She held out her arms and they embraced gently.

"Tee, I don't know what to say." He took both her hands in his and laughed. "I should have suspected you were too ornery to die." His laughter faded to a sad smile. "I missed you, Tee."

She nodded. "I know. I missed you, too, and I'm sorry. But it seemed best at the time." She paused. "You were happy, weren't you? I read that you and Caroline were married."

"For almost 40 years. She passed away several years ago. Now I keep busy with my children and grandchildren." He paused. "But you paid such a price, Tee."

"It's been a good life, Winston. I can honestly say I've enjoyed it thoroughly. I was never the Hollywood type. You know that. And I've made wonderful friends here." She remembered Addie suddenly and smiled at the young girl now.

"Here's one of them. Winston, I'd like you to meet Addie McCormick. Addie, Mr. Rinehart."

"Ah, yes, the young detective!"

Addie blushed. Winston laughed again and took her hand gently. "I believe Tee's met her match in you, dear. How do you do?" He bowed slightly and kissed her hand.

"How do you do," she stammered. "I better take some drinks to the table," she said and backed out of the door empty-handed.

She sped down the hall and into the dining room where her parents and the others were waiting. Mr. McCormick grinned at Addie's flushed face.

"Well, I'm glad to see I've given you a shock this time," he said. "Addie, this is Jack Krueger. I'm sure you remember Miss T. telling us of his help in her 'death.'"

Addie nodded and shook his outstretched hand. "Hi," she said.

"Addie, you're not going to believe how all this has turned out," Nick exclaimed. "Winston Rinehart works with a New York Museum as a consultant for their Theater Arts department. When your dad called Jack Krueger, Mr. Krueger offered to sell Miss T.'s mementos to the museum. Since he directed all the movies Rinehart and Bryce starred in, no one will wonder how he got hold of them. And Russ will act as his broker."

Addie glanced shyly at Russ and he grinned and winked at her.

"Hi, kid. Looks like we're finally on the same side."

She grinned back. "I'm glad—even though you did make a great villain!"

"Addie!" Mrs. McCormick was shocked, but Russ only laughed.

"Yeah," Nick agreed, "you sure added suspense to 'The Stranger in the Attic'."

"What?" Russ asked.

Just then Winston Rinehart and Miss T. joined the others at the table.

"We'll explain later," Addie said as they all sat down. "And who knows," she whispered in Nick's ear as they watched Rinehart and Bryce smile and laugh together, "there just might be a sequel!"

EPILOGUE

"I'm thankful for a lot of things"

The warm September sun shone brightly on the beautiful old mansion. Although it was Sunday and the yard was empty, there was evidence of activity everywhere you looked.

The once grey house was now painted a soft ivory, and the windows and doors were trimmed in complimentary tones of dark blue and beige. Scaffolding lined the west side of the house where the last group of new windows had yet to be installed on the third floor. The greenhouse, painted to match the mansion, still needed one section of roof replaced and there were ladders and shingles stacked beside it.

Large sections of the yard had been dug up and replanted with a variety of bulbs. Some had already bloomed and some would bloom the following spring. The symmetrical patches of fresh black dirt contrasted sharply with the dark green grass. A wrought-iron fence enclosed most of the yard and sparkling white gravel covered the entire drive.

Mr. McCormick whistled softly as they pulled up to the back door. "Miss T.'s certainly having the place fixed up right."

Addie nodded proudly. "And look at the greenhouse," she said. "We're going to have it ready for spring . . . March at the latest."

Mr. and Mrs. McCormick exchanged glances. "We?" her mother asked.

"It was Miss T.'s idea, Mom," Addie explained quickly. "She wants Nick and I to help with the garden next year."

"All right," her mother laughed. "Let me go see if Miss T.'s ready to leave."

The back door opened and Miss T. came down the steps. Mrs. McCormick moved to the back seat with Addie and Nick. Mr. McCormick held the car door for her, then helped Miss T. into the front seat.

The old woman began to fret as soon as they were on the road. "I can't believe I let you talk me into this," she said. She fussed with the gold chain around her neck, then patted her hair nervously. "I haven't set foot in a church for 50 years."

"Me neither," Nick muttered, and Addie giggled. He jabbed her with his elbow, although he couldn't help but grin. "You know what I mean."

"I think you'll be very comfortable in our church, Miss T. The people are wonderful. Besides, the children were eager for you to meet our guest speaker."

Malcolm Griffith was back in the area and had agreed to speak at their church that Sunday. Addie nudged Nick. "You can't tell me you're not as eager as I am to see Malcolm again."

"Yeah," Nick admitted, "I am looking forward to this."

"How are you and Amy getting along, Miss Tisdale?" Addie's mom changed the subject and Miss T. relaxed a little.

"That woman is a godsend!" she exclaimed and then clamped her mouth shut when she realized her choice of words. She glanced over the seat at Addie's smiling face. "I guess you won't argue with that, will you, miss? Anyway," she continued, " she hasn't got all her belongings moved in yet. It will take some time for her to get settled. But I want to thank you again for recommending her. She's a hard worker and we get along well. I don't trip over her every time I turn around, but she always seems to be there when I need her."

Miss T. had interviewed several women for the position of live-in companion, but none of them had filled her exacting requirements until she met Amy Takahashi. Amy was a widow and a volunteer at the radio station. Addie's mom was sure the two women would work well together and she had been right.

"Yes," Miss T. said, "I'm very thankful to have her. I'm . . . thankful for a lot of things," she added softly.

Addie breathed a deep sigh of contentment and closed her eyes. *So am I, Lord.*

Nick jabbed her in the side again. "Cut it out," he whispered.

"Cut what out?" she asked.

"Praying, that's what."

Addie just grinned. "Never!"

Other Good
Harvest House Reading

THE CRISTA CHRONICLES
by *Mark Littleton*

Secrets of Moonlight Mountain
When an unexpected blizzard traps Crista on Moonlight Mountain with a young couple in need of a doctor.

Winter Thunder
A sudden change in Crista's new friend, Jeff, and the odd circumstances surrounding Mrs. Oldham's broken windows all point to Jeff as the culprit in the recent cabin break-ins.

Robbers on Rock Road
When the clues fall into place regarding the true identity of the cabin-wreckers, Crista and her friends find themselves facing terrible danger!

Escape of the Grizzly
A grizzly is on the loose on Moonlight Mountain! Who will find the bear first—the sheriff's posse or the circus workers?

Danger on Midnight Trail
When Crista's dad is knocked unconscious on an overnight hike in the mountains, Crista and her cousin Sarah must find a way to get help.

BIBLE SEARCH SERIES
by *Sandy Silverthorne*

Bible stories have never been such fun! Jam-packed, over-sized pages burst with color and activity as author and illustrator Sandy Silverthorne takes kids on a treasure hunt through some of the best-loved Bible stories of all time.

> **The Great Bible Adventure**
> **The All-Time Awesome Bible Search**
> **In Search of Righteous Radicals**